JUST ONE LOOK

DARA GIRARD

ISBN: 978-1949764376

JUST ONE LOOK

Published by ILORI Press Books

ILORI PRESS BOOKS, LLC

P.O. Box 10332

Silver Spring, MD 20914

www.iloripressbooks.com

Table for Two

Gaining Interest

Careless Rapture

Dangerous Curves

Familiar Stranger

It Happened One Wedding

Unexpected Pleasure

Midnight Promise

Sweet Temptation

Always and Forever

Truly Yours

Clifton Sisters

The Sapphire Pendant

The Amber Stone

The Emerald Ring

Fortune Brothers

A Tempting Proposal

A Seductive Arrangement

Novels

Honest Betrayal

The Daughters of Winston Barnett

Remember My Name

Illusive Flame

Winterwood Lane

Promise Me

CHAPTER ONE

"Did you follow the instructions?"

"Of course I did," Caryn Chandler said as her best friend, Terri Reed, cut away the remnants of her hair.

"You probably used the wrong strength or left it in too long. This is not something you should do by yourself the night before an important event."

"I know that *now*," Caryn said as she watched more of her hair fall to the ground. Not that there was much left after her home perm had turned into a disaster. She usually went to the hair salon, but, just once, she wanted to do it herself. She wanted to look good at her niece's wedding the next day. And it had seemed so simple. Millions of women did it, why couldn't she? She was great at following directions and she'd checked each step twice. They were clear and straight forward. How hard could it be?

Obviously, harder than she thought because after applying the cream, waiting for it to take hold and straighten her hair, something went wrong. She still wasn't sure what. All she knew was that when she went to wash the cream out, her hair shouldn't have come out too. First there were just a few strands, then clumps, then handfuls. She'd screamed, wrapped her hair in a towel and called her friend who could barely understand her message.

Moments later, Terri, a small woman with smooth tan skin, arrived on her doorstep looking tired, the warm Friday evening behind her. "What are you talking about?"

Caryn took off her towel and showed her.

Terri's eyes widened. "Oh no."

"What should I do?"

"There's nothing you can do. We'll have to cut it."

Which was how they ended up in Caryn's bathroom trying to save what little hair Caryn had left on her head, her black, shoulder length hair now just a memory.

"Your sister is going to flip when she sees you," Terri said. "Maybe you should cancel."

"I can't cancel. What excuse would I give?"

"You can make up something."

"They're expecting me."

Terri shook her head and sighed. "What came over you?" She glanced around the pristine baby blue bathroom where the towels were lined up with precision, the toothbrush and paste sat with military-like perfection in a ceramic white cup. "This experiment is so unlike you."

"I just wanted to try something different. Peter thought I should shake up my routine a bit."

Terri rolled her eyes. "I don't know why you listen to

him. You're fine just the way you are."

Caryn glanced at her watch. "I wonder when the stores open."

"Why?"

"Because I have to buy a wig before Peter picks me up."

"You're taking him to the wedding?" Terri said, her voice cracking in surprise.

Caryn adjusted the blue towel around her shoulders. "Of course. He's my boyfriend and it's time he met my family."

"It's time he met any of us," Terri mumbled.

"He has a busy schedule."

That had always been his excuse—no reason, he liked to correct her—because he traveled a lot for his business—media relations for a digital firm—and when he got home he had to recuperate and didn't want to be around others. 'I'm so glad you understand me,' he always said with a smile. She also had to understand that because of his hectic schedule he tended to be forgetful. However, she'd reminded him three times about the upcoming wedding.

"Did you get your suit?" she'd asked him last week when they'd returned to her townhouse from a concert in the park.

"What suit?" he asked, pouring himself a glass of grape juice.

"For my niece's wedding," Caryn said, grabbing a sponge and wiping up the drops of grape juice that hadn't made it into the glass. "It's black tie."

He sat at the kitchen table, propping his feet up on another chair. She bristled at the motion but was glad at least she'd gotten him to take his shoes off. He always seemed to be sprawling somehow, he was tall, attractive, in a comfortable way, with reddish brown skin and dreds. "You have a niece old enough to get married?" he said.

"Yes, my sister's husband's daughter." *I've told you this before!* she wanted to say, but didn't. "She's really a step-niece but that doesn't matter."

He nodded. "Oh, yeah, right. Your sister's the one who married the old guy with money."

At forty-seven her sister's husband, Louis, wasn't exactly over the hill, but he was ten years older than her sister Ella and fifteen years older than Peter and herself. He'd come with two daughters from his previous marriage, but Caryn saw no distinction. She enjoyed being an aunt. And her niece's big day meant a lot to her. She wanted Peter to share the day with her. "So you'll get it tomorrow?"

"Get what?"

Caryn took a deep breath. "The suit."

"Don't worry I'll get it. You can be so uptight sometimes," he said, flashing a slow, sexy grin. "You need to learn to relax."

She did know how to relax, just not as much as he did. Most times he seemed as if he were sleep walking through life. His bedroom eyes and soft voice had initially attracted her. As a woman who was always alert, always scheduling things, he was a good contrast. He made her laugh. He helped her to slow down her pace, since she could be easily excitable, but at times his pace seemed glacial. It took four months before he agreed that they should be exclusive, six months before he let her see his place. Seven before he introduced her to a friend, the only one he seemed to have. A part time musician and full time bartender name "Muscle" (because he didn't appear to have any), who joked that Caryn was too good for Peter. Sometimes she wondered if he had really been joking.

Peter got looks wherever he went. He had a laidback air—like a man lazing on a Caribbean beach, possibly high on something—that seemed to draw women to him. Many times at a restaurant he seemed to be looking past her, not at someone else, just in another space. 'Lost in thought,' he'd say. Or 'I'm paid to think so I can't help myself.' And she learned not to mind. At least she tried to. She didn't mind the faraway looks, the causal grins, the slow pace, the 'don't worry so much, babe', but she hated when he forgot things. She had a drawer filled with wasted theater tickets and cancelled reservations and many memories of missed dinners and forgotten dates. And each time he'd smile and kiss her, tell her how sorry he was and buy her something or make it up to her in bed.

But this time she didn't want excuses or make up sex. She'd sent him text reminders. Put the wedding date on his digital calendar, so that he'd get an alert, and marked it on his favorite calendar in his bedroom, where a picture of a beautiful woman straddled a yellow Ferrari in a way that didn't seem feasible. She'd not give him an excuse. She'd even shown him her dress two days ago.

"You look good," he said, admiring the spaghetti strap dark purple dress as he sat in her living room. "What's the occasion?"

She paused. "My niece's wedding."

He snapped his fingers and nodded. "Oh yeah, right. The bride better watch out."

It was a corny joke, but she decided to let it pass. She knew she looked good, but not as good as a beaming twenty-two year old bride who wore a size two. "So are you ready?" she asked him.

He rubbed his eyes and yawned. "Ready for what?"

"The wedding."

He frowned. "What wedding?"

"The wedding we're going to in three days."

He nodded again. "Oh yeah, that."

"Please tell me you got a suit."

He stood up and wrapped his arms around her waist. "Don't worry, babe." He kissed her. "I'll get to it."

She stiffened. "You shouldn't wait until the last minute."

"It's not the last minute." He grinned. "You said I have three days."

"Maybe I should go with you today." She pulled out her mobile phone. "We could—"

"Sorry," he said, placing a kiss on her shoulder. "I've got things I have to do."

"But—"

"I'll get the suit." He kissed her other bare shoulder. "Relax."

His touch felt good, but his words made her nervous. How could she relax when he should have gotten his suit days ago? "And you're supposed to pick me up. We can't be late."

"We won't be late. You know I don't do things the

way you do, you'll just have to trust me." He wrapped his arms tighter. "Don't you trust me?"

Only sometimes. "Yes."

"That's my girl." He released his hold and playfully slapped her on the bottom. "You need to loosen up a bit. If you're not careful you can sound like a nag."

His words hurt. She didn't think she was nagging him. She didn't expect him to schedule every minute the way she did, or to get tasks done months before they were due, but she had hoped that he would at least understand how much this day meant to her. She wanted him to show a little interest in finally meeting her family and friends. But maybe that was unfair. Few things excited him. He wasn't a man who showed a lot of emotion. He was even-keeled like an ocean at rest, unlike her ex, Adrian, who...no that was years ago and she didn't want to think about him.

Maybe that was why she'd messed up her perm. She'd been so eager to prove that she wasn't a nag, that she could be as nonchalant as him, that she hadn't followed the instructions perfectly. Sometimes his lackadaisical mood made her wonder if they truly were a good match. But she believed she learned a lot from him and vice versa.

"I don't think we'll have enough time to get you a good wig," Terri said, setting the scissors down.

"I saw a place with plenty."

"It's not that simple. You don't just go in and pick something off of a mannequin head. You want good quality and to be fitted."

"You're right. I don't have time for that. I just need something that will pass."

EARLY THE NEXT MORNING, Caryn went shopping and found a slick, light brown wig with bangs, back home she changed into her dress and waited for Peter in her living room, imaging what he'd look like in his suit.

And waited, wondering if she should have chosen to give the new couple a different gift.

And waited, hoping that Peter hadn't forgotten the time he was supposed to pick her up.

And waited until she was certain that he had.

She called him. When he didn't picked up. She texted him.

WHERE ARE YOU?

Seconds later he replied, WHY?

THE WEDDING!

SH** WAS THAT TODAY?

She gripped the phone, imaging it was his neck, and shook it. *You idiot!* She took a deep breath before she called him. This time he picked up. "You know it was today!" she said before he could speak.

"Right. Sorry. Things got a little crazy and—"

She paced. "Crazy? You don't know crazy. I'm going crazy right now."

"I didn't mean—"

She stopped in front of a window, staring up at the cloudless spring sky. "You werc supposed take me."

"I'll shower and change and grab something to wear."

"You can't just *grab* something, you were supposed to rent a suit!"

"Listen, babe. It's no big deal. I'll just—"

She watched a sparrow land on a thin branch of a dogwood tree, causing white petals to fall on the lawn and in the road. "It is a big deal."

"Do you want me to meet your family or not?"

A car sped down the street, smashing the petals into the ground. "Yes, but—"

"Then you have to take me as I am. We'll be a little late, but—"

"Forget it." Caryn hung up, blinking back tears of anger. She turned off the ringer when the phone rang. She didn't want to talk to him. She should have gotten the suit for him. She should have had it hanging on his closet door with notes about when to put it on, when to pick her up. But the truth was, he'd disappointed her for the last time.

She wiped her tears and reapplied her makeup then grabbed her purse and keys and got in her car. She wouldn't let him ruin her mood. It was the perfect day for a wedding.

Just as she started the ignition, she got a call from her sister.

The special ringtone she'd given her sister always made her smile. "Don't worry," she said once she answered. "I'll be right there—"

"I'm not calling about that. I need your help."

"Why?"

"The wedding planner double booked the reception hall."

CHAPTER TWO

Two hours.

She was supposed to make a miracle happen—create a stress free, beautiful wedding reception to accommodate one hundred guests—in two hours.

Caryn met briefly with the wedding planner, a friend of her niece's who looked ready to burst into tears, and the hotel manager where the reception was to be held. She discovered that while the large meeting room was no longer available, a small meeting room which opened into a small alcove, with a private fenced in garden area with awnings would work as a backup. The hotel manager promised to provide the tables, chairs and basic covering, in addition to two portable bars that could be used on either side of the venue. He also agreed to call in several wait staff to help, and suggested a buffet-style set up instead of a sit down.

Caryn also met with the chef, who assured her that the food would not be a problem. He could accommodate her, for a price, which she was willing to pay. The main areas she needed to focus on were the decorations and entertainment. Fortunately, because her niece had relied so heavily on the wedding planner, and had not taken any notice of what had been planned for the reception, Caryn knew that whatever she came up with would work, as long as it was a success.

She glanced at the clock seeing the minutes clicking down to when everything had to be ready. She called a neighbor of hers, who had two teenage sons, basketball players. Her offer of fifty dollars for one hour of work was enough temptation and resulted in her getting the services of five strapping young men to help with the decorations. She recruited Terri to help her by going to a nearby craft store and getting a supply of satin ribbon, crepe paper and an assortment of glass bowls. Caryn called a local florist and begged them to deliver whatever fresh flowers they had available. They surprised her with two large bouquets of cream colored roses which she placed on either side of the doorway, and an assortment of flowers, for use as centerpieces.

Since she planned on a buffet-style setting, she didn't have to worry about name plates and seating arrangements, except for the main table to host the bride and groom and their parents. Caryn used the satin ribbon to make a creative design for the head table, twining the ribbon over the table and around the legs. She created small flower baskets bursting with white lilies, callas, and poms surrounded by lush green using the small centerpieces the florist sent and the extra ribbon to hang them along the awning, creating a festive atmosphere.

By the time the guests arrived, lights sparkled along the bushes and walls enclosing the area, crepe paper in pastel colors, were shaped and formed to look like large billowing petals, creating an elegant backdrop where the buffet stood. The two portable bars were used for the refreshments and a cupcake station, where guests could pick up a piece of the wedding cake, and add a topping, if they wanted, before having the item wrapped in plastic if they opted to take a piece home, instead of eating it there.

Since there was really no room for dancing, Caryn called in a favor from a friend who was a member of a steel pan group, who agreed to provide the music.

Near the end of the evening, Caryn flopped into a chair, amazed she'd been able to pull it off, when she noticed her earring underneath a chair. She got down on her knees and reached for it, but before she could straighten, she felt a huge weight jump on her back and cry, "Horsy!"

She knew by the tone that it was her four year old nephew, Dean, who was sweet, talkative and twenty pounds heavier than he should be, since his parents indulged him with sugary treats.

"No, now is not the time to play," she said.

"I want to play."

"Get down."

"Horsy." He nudged her on the sides as if she were a horse. "Get up."

"Don't make Aunty angry."

Before she had to get too stern with him, she suddenly felt the weight lifted. She turned and saw Dean being carried by a man, but only saw the man's back. He carried the child with ease, which was an amazing feat, and had whispered something in his ear that made the boy's dimples show, before he set him down and the child ran off. But that wasn't the only reason she stared at him. There was something familiar about him. The shape of his shoulders, the cut of his hair, the scent of his cologne. That scent reminded her of warm autumn nights and candlelight; cold beer and hot hands sliding down her body.

Caryn swallowed, resisting the urge to fan herself, her cheeks burning. *Where had that thought come from?* This feeling was completely unlike her. She hadn't had such a strong reaction to a man since...but no... It couldn't be him.

In seconds the helpful stranger was gone and she almost felt she'd imagined it. A silent hero. She hadn't gotten a chance to thank him.

"You're a miracle worker," her sister, Ella, said. She wore a saucy little hat, which matched her pink dress that was poised daintily on her perfectly styled hair. Caryn had helped her sister shop for the perfect mother-of-the-bride dress so she wouldn't be out done by Louis' first wife, who'd arrived in a striking, lace-patterned dress. They both shared their father's medium build and dark toffee colored skin, but Ella had their mother's trim figure and dainty nose, while Caryn inherited her grandmother's square jaw and wide mouth.

Ella glanced up. "Should I even ask about your hair?"

"No."

"It doesn't matter anyway. You've done so much," Ella said, her hand shaking as she adjusted her hat.

"What now?" Caryn asked, noticing the motion and the worry in her sister's eyes.

"He's here."

Caryn put her earring back in place. "Who's here?"

"At least, I think it's him." Ella bit her lip. "It might not be."

"Who?"

Her sister waved a dismissive hand. "It's probably nothing. He probably just looks like him. Never mind. It likely wasn't him. It's been so long and he had a goatee."

"Who?" Caryn asked, losing patience.

Ella glanced around then lowered her voice. "I thought I saw...Adrian."

"What!"

"But it was just a brief glimpse so I could be wrong," she said in a rush. "It's been so many years. Caryn please don't look like that. I'm probably wrong. I'm sorry I even brought it up."

Caryn felt blood drain from her face. "You think he's here?"

"I'm not sure. I'm sure it wasn't him. Forget I said anything."

How could she forget? Adrian? Could he be here? Would she see him again after eight years? She thought of the man who'd helped remove Dean. Was it him? No, it couldn't be. He probably would have laughed and said it served her right.

If she hadn't run out on him they would have been married eight years by now. Maybe have a child or two. But she had and there was no point looking back.

"YOU KNOW you've only dated losers since...it happened," Terri said when Caryn told her about the reception, since Terri hadn't stayed after helping Caryn set up, and the end of her relationship with Peter. Caryn sat crossed legged on her bed while Terri trimmed Caryn's wig.

"I don't know what you mean."

"Peter was a loser in a long line of losers. It's as if you're punishing yourself because of..." she let her words fade away, but her silence spoke volumes.

Caryn stretched her legs out. Even since college, Terri hadn't been one to beat around the bush and the trait served her well as the executive manager of CCQ—Clutter Cleanup Queens—a female owned company that helped put together teams to help hoarders. "My mistake with Peter has nothing to do with what happened in the past."

"What would you say if you saw him again?"

"I never want to."

"But what if?"

"Besides 'I'm sorry,' what is there to say?" *And I may have seen him again,* but she didn't feel comfortable admitting that. What if she was wrong? What did it matter now?

"You have to forgive yourself."

"I have."

"By dating a jerk like Peter?"

"You never met him."

"I didn't have to meet him to know what he's like. All

that you told me was enough. This last fiasco just proves it. Before him was DoughBoy."

"His name was—"

Terri covered her ears. "I don't care." She let her hands fall to her lap. "All I remember was that he was boring and dull, and did I say boring?"

"He was just intellectual."

"And I'm not?"

"You know I didn't mean that."

"That jerk put you down every chance he could."

"Let's not talk about my past. I'm taking a breather from men for a while. I have a new client and opportunity."

Caryn looked forward to expanding the reach of her business, Simple Life Services, which helped people get organized. She'd passed the crucial five year mark and was starting to get more business through referrals rather than having to constantly drum up new business through her popular blog and column in a local Home and Garden ezine.

Terri styled Caryn's wig. "Maybe you should reschedule."

"Why would I do that?"

Terri set the wig down. "I just don't think the stars are aligned for you."

"I don't believe in that."

"It doesn't matter. You've had two major things happen this week and a third one is coming. I really think—"

"If bad things happen in threes then they've already

happened. My hair fell out, my boyfriend turned into a toad—"

"He was already a toad," Terri mumbled.

"And my niece's reception was nearly a disaster."

Terri shook her head. "I have this strange feeling that something big is going to happen."

"I'll be fine." Caryn put on another wig.

Her friend looked at her and frowned. "You're not wearing that."

"What's wrong with it?"

"It looks like a wig."

"Probably because it is one. I got a two for one deal."

"And you're bragging about it?"

"I thought it was nice of the sales clerk."

"She was just unloading stock. Why didn't you wait for me to go with you?"

"You're busy and I thought I could get this taken care of. And hey!" she cried when Terri yanked the wig off her head.

"You're not wearing this—ever."

"Fine." Caryn said, trying the first one on again. She stared at herself in her closet mirror. "This looks good."

"I wish you'd listen to me and cancel. I really have a bad feeling about this." She paused. "Okay, maybe it's not a bad feeling exactly but that something major is about to happen to you."

"It's just a new client. What could possibly go wrong?"

CHAPTER THREE

It wasn't the first time Caryn had fallen in love. But it was the first time she'd fallen in love with a place and so quickly. Within seconds of being in her new client's apartment her heart raced, her palms felt hot, her breathing quickened. Her body responded to every corner and wall. The apartment burst with warmth and personality. The location, in one of Maryland's most expensive zip codes, and size—a living room the size of an Olympic pool—alone told her the occupant made a lot of money and could afford her most exclusive services. Caryn eagerly looked around the apartment, her mind already bright with ideas, as she gathered clues about the occupant. Her gaze scanned over the yellow and black stripped piano that stood in the main room and the saxophone case in the corner, the scattered music sheets on a side table, the music stand, and books on music theory, top performers and music history made it clear the instruments weren't just for show: They were a passion.

The occupant also liked martial arts. She noticed a black belt folded on a bookshelf next to a book on akido and silhouettes of a jai alai master in four different stances. The space was more cluttered than filthy, which made her job easy. She could organize it in no time. The only thing that surprised her was that the muted colors of the room and heavy furniture seemed to suit a more masculine taste than the pretty woman sitting in front of her in the living room. Nothing seemed to fit Caryn's impression of Roberta Johnston, a reserved and calm woman wearing dark rimmed glasses, a prim dark green blouse, and dark blue jeans.

Caryn knew Roberta was a top videographer, so she evidently had a creative side to her, but her personality didn't seem to be in the place. Not even the collection of teddy bears, taking up an entire side of the apartment, which seemed to have swallowed the space as if they'd been carried in by a tidal wave, appeared to suit her. But she wasn't one to judge. People had many different sides.

"Let me guess," Caryn said with a smile. "I'm here about the teddy bears."

"Yes. This is my boyfriend's place and his sister's the cofounder of an organization that donates these items to shelters, hospitals and nursing homes."

So that's it! Caryn felt relieved, but the feeling didn't last long. "This isn't your place?"

"No, but it's okay. He's very laidback about these things. He told me that I could help him get organized and since I don't know much, I thought I'd call in the professionals."

"That's admirable, but I really think he should be

here to make the decision." Plus she wanted to meet him, just out of curiosity, to see if her impression of him was correct. In her mind she'd already created a picture of him. As a default, she imagined he was black, like his girlfriend, and fit, with long fingers. He preferred T-shirts and jeans over suits and ties, but could clean up well. Unlike some clients, he would be malleable to change and from the sight of the piano had a quirky sense of humor and style.

"He's busy," Roberta said, making it clear Caryn wouldn't get a chance to see him. "And he trusts me."

Caryn tried another tactic. "But I'd like to know more about him. It's a wonderful space and if it reflects him in any way I'd love a chance to meet him."

Roberta glanced around the apartment with affection. "What you see is what you get, really. He shouldn't have taken on this extra job, but he hates letting people down. He owns a bunch of businesses."

"Did you say business*es*?"

"Yes," Roberta said with a nod, "but he's not a workaholic." She nodded to his saxophone. "He likes to jam with friends and is very easy going. There's nothing you could do to make him angry, so don't worry. The only thing that gets him nervous are small spaces." She rolled her eyes. "It still takes me forever to get him to use elevators, but he's improving. Anyway, just tell me what you think we should do. I'd really like to surprise him."

He sounded wonderful. Perfect. Even his little eccentricities. Plus his place seemed to fill all her senses, the bright grayish-green of the succulent on his windowsill, the smell of wood, the soft feel of the cloth covered couch. There was something warm and familiar about his place. She felt an odd sense of déjà vu, although she'd never been in the apartment before. She envied Roberta, wanting to ask where she'd found her boyfriend. Did he have friends? A single brother? But after Peter, any new relationship would be rebound hell, so she pushed her curiosity aside and said, "Okay, then we can get started."

Before Roberta could reply the loud wailing of a rock guitar solo drifted in from another room. She rolled her eyes, "I don't know why he keeps doing that."

"What is it?"

She stood. "It's his alarm. He always sets it wrong. I don't know why. He'll set it for evening instead of day, or seconds instead of minutes. It's real strange."

Caryn laughed. "I used to know someone who did that."

"Did they ever improve?"

"No."

Roberta sighed as a heavy drum beat met with the sound of a wailing guitar. "I'll be back in a minute."

Caryn sat back and looked around the apartment again. She was about to stand when Roberta's cell phone rang. She sent it a cursory glance, then paused and looked at it again in disbelief. She saw an image on the screen that made her freeze. A face she hadn't seen in eight years. A handsome male face smiling: Adrian.

What was he doing on Roberta's phone?

The phone quickly went quiet. Caryn swallowed. What should she do? Tell her about the call? Pretend it hadn't happened? Get out of there?

Roberta sat back down then noticed a message on her phone. "Oh damn. I'll call him back in a minute."

Oh no. Caryn thought, looking around the room with new eyes. Now she knew why everything seemed so familiar. It was *his* place. The décor had changed from the struggling entrepreneur he'd been, but the essence was the same. And now she remembered that book on music—the tiny black and white photo of a suspension bridge, the martial art silhouettes.

"Who, uh, called?" Caryn asked, knowing it was none of her business, but hoping Roberta would tell her that the man on the screen was a work colleague or a relative or someone else completely. Maybe he was just a lookalike.

"My boyfriend. Adrian." She held up the phone. "Isn't he handsome?"

Caryn could only make a strangling noise in her throat. Terri had been right. She'd warned her not to take the job. Why hadn't she listened?

Soon they heard footsteps and a key in the door. Roberta swore. "That's him. He wasn't supposed to be home yet."

Caryn's heart began to race. She had to disappear. She couldn't see him. But there was nowhere to hide. "Um...where's your bathroom?"

"Down the hall and—"

Caryn didn't give Roberta a chance to finish. She grabbed her purse, raced into the bathroom and closed the door. Why was this happening? Why did it have to be his place? Why did she run? She should have stayed and said hello and then made her exit. It would have been awkward, but more mature. She still could behave like an adult. She could fix her makeup, take a deep breath, then face him again.

Caryn opened her handbag and pulled out her lipstick. She went to the mirror and started to apply it then stopped. No, she couldn't face him. Not looking like this. Suddenly, her jacket looked tired and old fashioned, her makeup bland. In comparison to Roberta, she looked...dull, and that was saying a lot.

A square bottle of cologne peeked out the side of his medicine cabinet. Her heart began to pound at the sight of it, triggering memories that sent her senses spinning. She knew how the earthy, woodsy scent on his skin could drive her wild. She put her lipstick away, grabbed the bottle and opened it then closed her eyes and sniffed it, remembering one fantasy she'd had of soaking her finger inside the cologne then rubbing it all over his body. His beautiful, brown, body.

Her eyes flew open, her heart pounding even faster than before. *What was she doing? Why was she thinking this way?*

She quickly replaced the bottle, nearly dropping it, and shut the cabinet. She'd be adult another day. Not now. Not when she wasn't thinking straight.

But what should she do? She looked around annoyed by the faint scent of his cologne that now clung to her fingers; that she noticed he still bought yellow toothbrushes. "If I want a bright smile, I've gotta use a bright color," he used to say. And he would smile at her and make her heart melt every time. Caryn inwardly groaned. She didn't want to remember that.

She didn't want to remember how much fun they'd had together.

She had to get out!

She saw the window near the shower. A window! That would be her escape. She lifted it and looked down. Two floors. She could make it.

Caryn tossed her handbag out the window then crawled out. She grabbed the ledge, said a small prayer then let go. The ground met her faster than she'd expected, and she felt stabbing through her ankle as it twisted at an odd angle, but that was it. She was still in one piece. She was free. She just needed to make it to her car.

Caryn rose to her feet, limped over to the parking lot and stopped when two worn sneakers came into view.

"What are you doing?"

She knew that voice. That deep, low rumble. A voice that reminded her of whiskey over rocks and a low tide. She hadn't heard it in eight years, but it hadn't changed.

Fate. I hate you. Why hadn't his apartment been higher up? Then she would be dead and she wouldn't have to face him. She wouldn't look up at him. She'd pretend he was a stranger. She didn't have to explain herself to strangers.

"A neighbor called because she saw someone sneaking out of my apartment," he continued.

Somebody saw her? She quickly lifted her head and to her horror saw a small gathering of people—a small group of preschoolers linked hand in hand, and an older couple in matching jogging suits, a teenager on a skateboard, an expensively dressed woman with a cell phone.

Why hadn't she seen them before? Had they taken pictures?

"I'm sorry," she said, being careful not to look at his face. She kept her gaze lowered, which was a mistake because it focused directly on his chest. His fit, wide chest. His fit, wide, muscular chest. The white T-shirt seeming to emphasis every contour. He was beautifully made and that hadn't changed. She shifted her gaze to the ground again. That was better. His shoes. She'd stare at his shoes. His big, well worn shoes. There was nothing sexy about a man's shoes, except that she used to tease him about his big feet and hands. She's learned to stop teasing him about them in bed when he showed her how well he used them...

Roberta's voice of concern interrupted her dangerous, wayward thoughts. "Caryn? Are you okay?"

No, I'm slowly dying of embarrassment. "I'm fine."

Roberta came to her side and lowered her voice. "I know I said I wanted to keep this a surprise, but I didn't expect you to try to disappear. I didn't realize you were so dedicated."

"Yes, that's me," she said, wishing she had a hole to crawl into. "Didn't want to spoil the surprise."

"You are so sweet." She turned to him. "Adrian, I want to explain."

"No, you really don't need to," Caryn said. "Let's discuss this later."

"I hired her to help you organize. I know I said I'd do it myself, but I thought I'd hire a professional. I was going to have her do all the work and take all the credit. That's why she was trying to escape."

Adrian made a noncommittal sound deep in his throat then said, "Is that right Ms.—?"

"Chandler," Roberta said. "Her name is Caryn Chandler."

But of course you already know that.

"A pleasure to meet you." He held out his hand.

"I would shake hands," Caryn said, balling them into fists. She couldn't touch him. Wouldn't. "But mine are filthy. I should go."

"But we didn't finish the consultation and now that Adrian's here you can get his ideas. She really loved your place," Roberta said, addressing Adrian, "and wanted to get to know you better."

"How much better?" Adrian asked.

"I'll get back to you on that." Caryn headed towards her car. "Excuse me."

"You're limping," Roberta said, following her.

She gritted her teeth. Her ankle burned, but humiliation made the pain bearable. "I'm fine."

"You should get that looked at."

"I will."

Before Roberta could make another suggestion her mobile phone rang. "I have to get this. Bye, Caryn. Talk to you again."

Caryn waved without looking back and kept walking. Why had she parked so far away? Why did she still feel his gaze on her?

"Caryn?"

He was following her? Why wouldn't he leave her alone? Why did the sound of her name on his lips make her skin tingle? "Don't worry, I'll quit and I won't tell her why."

"CeCe?"

He had no right to call her that. He was the only one who ever used that nickname, but then again he was the one who had given it to her, using her first and last initial to come up with a name that tied them together with memories. How dare he remember it now.

"Hold on a minute," he said approaching her.

"She doesn't know anything about us and I didn't know about you. If I had, I wouldn't have come. I didn't touch anything."

He grabbed her wrist. "Will you just stop for a minute?"

She squeezed her eyes shut. He was touching her and she should break away. She shouldn't remember how strong and warm his grip was. How tenderly he used to hold her. His palm felt hot on her skin as if he were branding her and making her his. *Please don't mention the past, please don't say anything.* "I just need to get to my car. I have another appointment and I have to wrap my ankle before I get there."

"I don't want to stop you, there's just something you need to know."

Why did he have to smell so good? Why did he make her want to slowly undo his buttons one-by-one? Caryn took a deep breath then spun around and looked up at him. Another mistake. Just as she'd fallen in love with his apartment, she felt herself falling in love with him all over again. The goatee was the only difference. He still had his sensual full lips, compelling brown eyes, and square jaw. She nervously licked her lips. He wanted to tell her something important; she could see it in his gaze. Did he feel it too? This connection she'd fought to break all those years ago?

"What do you want to tell me?" she said, her voice sounding breathier than she'd hoped.

He held her gaze for a long moment, then said, "Your wig is crooked."

CHAPTER FOUR

"Are you sure it was him?" Terri asked, leaning forward, tucking a strand of hair behind her ear.

They sat in their favorite café where Terri made her way through an iced strudel and black tea, while Caryn's black coffee and croissant remained untouched. After leaving Adrian, she'd called her friend to meet her after work to commiserate. She didn't want to go home.

Caryn folded her arms and looked at her.

"Sorry, silly question." She took a sip of tea. "Are you sure he remembered you?"

Caryn just lifted a brow.

Terri sat back. "Okay, point taken."

"He looked better than ever and I'm..." Caryn looked down at herself and she let her words fade away.

"You're fine. You look great."

Caryn pulled off her wig. "I'm amazed how you can say that with a straight face."

Terri leaped up and replaced the wig. "What is

wrong with you?" she demanded glancing around the café in case anyone saw.

"I don't care who sees me. This has been one of the worst days of my life."

"Your hair will grow back and most people gain a little weight as they get older. And you're focusing on your business so much you haven't paid attention to your clothes."

Caryn paused. "What's wrong with my clothes?"

Terri hesitated. "You're the one who brought up your looks."

"I wasn't talking specifically about my clothes. What do you think is wrong with them? Honestly."

"They're a little out of date."

"Anything else you think I should change?"

"No, except..."

"Except what?"

"You need to learn how to have a little more fun. You've gotten really serious lately. If you're not careful you could turn into your aunt."

Caryn shivered at the thought. "You think I should give Peter another chance?"

"No," Terri said quickly, as if horrified by the idea. "You did the right thing, but...never mind. What are you going to do?"

"I'm going to tell her to find someone else. I already told him I'd quit."

"What did he say?"

"He didn't say anything." Not that she'd given him a chance to. After his comment about her wig, she'd gotten into her car and driven away.

"Maybe this is a good thing."

"How can it be good?"

"Seeing him again may help you to get over him."

Caryn took a bite of her croissant. "I am over him."

"Then why did you run?"

"Because I was caught by surprise. I thought I'd never have to see him again."

"And now that you have, what do you feel?"

"Besides embarrassed, humiliated, and devastated?"

"Yes. You were scared about seeing him again and now that you have, how do you feel?"

That I wish I hadn't let him go. "Nothing. I've moved on, but first I have to tell Roberta I'm not taking the job."

"WHY DIDN'T YOU TELL ME?" Roberta said, playfully slapping Caryn on the arm.

They sat in Adrian's living room where a giant teddy bear sat in the corner. She hadn't seen it there last time and she didn't want to be there, but Roberta had been insistent and Caryn knew the only way to break things off was to be as amenable as possible. She'd tried to broach the subject over the phone, but Roberta wouldn't let her, telling her how excited she was to be working together. She thought of ending the project by email, but all variations sounded cold and petty. She wanted to leave a good impression, in case Roberta knew of others who'd make great references, so she decided to meet her one last time on the condition that Adrian wasn't there. Roberta assured her that he wouldn't be, so Caryn sat in the familiar room, wondering the best way to end things.

Caryn absently rubbed her arm, surprised by the strength of Roberta's playful teasing. "Tell you what?"

"I'm so glad to see your ankle's better."

"Tell you what?" Caryn repeated.

"That you'd met Adrian before?"

She stiffened. *He told you about us? Did he tell you what I did to him?* "I didn't think it was important."

"He said you'd changed so much he'd hardly recognized you."

Ouch. Score one for him. But he was right. At thirty-two she wasn't the young woman she'd been eight years ago. She was heavier, not as stylish and now she hardly had any hair. *Bet you're glad you didn't marry me, then, huh?* "He's changed too," Caryn said, just to say something even though it was a lie. He hadn't changed in the ways she had. He'd become more successful, and better looking. If that was possible.

Roberta adjusted her glasses. "But he didn't tell me much more than that. Just that you shared a mutual friend or something."

"Yes, that's right."

Roberta bit her lip. "Can I be honest?"

No, lie to me. "Sure."

"He doesn't seem to like you very much. He doesn't think you're right for this job."

Ouch. Score two. But he was right. "Which is why I wanted to have this discussion with you. I think it's best that you select—"

Roberta pointed at her. "So I told him, that I don't

care what happened between you two in the past, that you're one of the best organizers I've heard about and I wanted to use you."

"That's very kind of you but—"

"And then he said you're not trustworthy—"

"Well he may—"

"And I said—"

"I think you should listen to him," Caryn said, losing patience.

"Why?" Roberta narrowed her eyes. "You're not trustworthy?"

Caryn shook her head. "No, that's not it, but there's bad blood between us and—"

Roberta learned forward her eyes glittering with interest. "What did you do to him?" She lowered her voice. "Sleep with his best friend? I did that once, but didn't get caught. Thank you, God," she said, making a quick sign of the cross.

"You slept with Ken?"

Roberta's eyes widened. "You know his best friend? Isn't he a doll?"

That's not my question! "Yes, but I didn't mean—"

"Should I tell him you said hello?"

No! Are you crazy? "That wouldn't be appropriate. I'm just surprised that...I just didn't think he was the type to..." Caryn shook her head, trying to get her mind in order. Roberta had slept with Ken? Temperamental Ken Tagawa, the proud third generation Brazilian who was often mistaken for Japanese? A man whose spot on impressions of world leaders used to leave her aching with laughter and who could swear in seven languages?

That Ken? "It's none of my business if you want to be with him."

Roberta stared at her for a moment then laughed. "No, I didn't cheat on Adrian with Ken." She laughed harder. "As if that would ever happen. Although he does have a certain allure," she said with a grin. "But no...I've never seen two men so devoted to each other. I think they'd dump any woman who tried to come between them."

"Hmm."

"No, before I was referring to my ex-boyfriend. When you've got a guy like Adrian, you don't even think about stepping out on him. He meets all your needs and more if you know what I mean."

Caryn rubbed the bridge of her nose. Why was she having this conversation? "Well, I'm happy for both of you, but as I was saying—"

"I was just joking with you about cheating. You don't seem the type, but is it Ken?"

She let her hand fall to her lap. "Is what Ken? I don't—"

"Your mutual friend?"

Why wouldn't this woman let her finish a sentence? "Sort of but—"

"I don't mean to pry, but did you break Ken's heart or something, because Adrian usually likes people, but he doesn't seem to like you."

"No I didn't break Ken's heart. The truth is—"

Roberta held up her hand. "You don't have to say anything. I already know."

What! "You know?"

"I don't know the details of course, but I can guess. You two can't stand each other because you're so different. Complete opposites. I can see someone like you grating on his nerves and vice versa. You're like oil and water, cats and dogs. But," Roberta continued before Caryn could correct her, "he doesn't understand that I need someone like you. I told him that he didn't have to be around when we worked on this project, and that it wouldn't take long, so he can just deal with it. So that's that."

You two would never get on. But eight years ago they'd been inseparable. She'd imagined spending the rest of her life with him. How wrong she'd been. "I think you should take his feelings into consideration."

"I have and I decided that I'm working with you."

"But it's his place."

"I know what's best for him. I told him to stay away until we're done so you don't have to worry about bumping into him again. You told me this project wouldn't take more than a couple days at most. And I won't take no for an answer. Okay?"

No, it wasn't okay, but a woman like Roberta was like a steamroller. She'd get her way one way or another. Since he'd stay away, Caryn wouldn't have to see him so she could do the project. She was over him and he was over her. "Okay, but I'll complete the project in one day and I'll do it for free."

CHAPTER FIVE

"Free!" Terri screeched over the phone. "You'll do a big project like that for nothing?!"

Caryn washed her dinner dishes and set them aside to dry. "She wouldn't listen to anything else. And I don't want to take his money. I can't believe he's with a woman like that. She's all wrong for him. You should have heard her go on about how he couldn't tell her what to do. I mean you think she should take his feelings into account with something like this. If he'd told me there was someone he didn't want me to work with I would at least consider it. That's what a girlfriend does."

"Oh no."

"What?"

"You're still in love with him," Terri said in a grave tone.

Caryn laughed. "What?"

"Don't laugh, this is serious."

"No, it's not."

"You haven't stopped talking about her for nearly thirty minutes."

Caryn pulled off her gloves. "That doesn't mean I'm still in love with him. I just can't believe this is the woman he's chosen. She wouldn't let me finish a sentence. She assumed I'd never cheat on a man."

"You wouldn't."

Caryn left the kitchen and flopped into a chair in her living room. "But what gives her the right to assume that? To assume that she knows me? To assume that Adrian and I would make a terrible couple? You should have heard her going on about how much Adrian and I would be a bad match. How opposite we are. How different we are."

"And she's right."

She moved a coaster on her coffee table slightly to the left to make it look more balanced. "We were a great couple. We had a lot of fun." She pushed the coaster slightly to the right. "Others didn't see what we had."

"Then why didn't you marry him?" Terri asked in a quiet voice.

She frowned, the coaster still looked a little off balance. She moved it to the left again. "Because marriage would have been a mistake," she said, using the same reason she'd convinced herself to believe in the past.

"No, I'll tell you why. It's because your Aunt Barbara convinced you that Adrian was all wrong and you got scared and you gave up a great love. And seeing him again you know what you lost and it's killing you."

Caryn picked up the coaster and tossed it across the room. "I don't want to talk about it."

"That's all you've been talking about whether you want to admit it or not. He's over you, but you're not over him. You can't do this job free or otherwise. You have to stay away."

"No," she said, standing to retrieve the coaster from where it had landed in the corner. "I have to do this." She put the coaster back in place. "I have to close this chapter in my life." She drummed her fingers on the coffee table. The coaster wasn't perfect, but she'd have to let it be. "Maybe it's a just punishment."

"Don't you think you've punished yourself enough?"

She took a deep breath shifted the coaster one last time then said, "No, I ran away from him twice. I won't do it again."

YOU STILL LOVE HIM. It was stupid. It was crazy. It was wrong. But it was the truth. Just one look at him and she was lost. He'd stolen her heart and she'd never gotten in back. But it's too late! Her heart said. There was nothing she could do about it now. This was her punishment. She'd left him. She'd hurt him. Isn't this what she'd wished for him? That's he'd go on with his life and be happy? And he was happy with a new woman. She still thought she was wrong for him, but she wasn't the best judge on relationships.

She'd focused so much on her work since leaving him. She'd made it her life, but she didn't want that life anymore. She wanted...

She sighed. She wasn't exactly sure.

"Listen lady if you can't pay then you have to leave."

Caryn looked at the dark haired older woman in a peach linen jacket with precise hawk-like features who stood in the checkout line in front of her. A little girl of about two slept in the grocery cart's child's seat, her forehead resting on the handlebar. The older woman had gone through two credit cards and both had been declined.

"She's with me," Caryn said smoothly. "Just put her total with mine."

The woman's dark gaze looked at her in awe. "But—"

"No, buts. Enjoy the rest of your day."

The woman thanked her then left.

"It could be a scam you know," the clerk said, a young man with a tattoo of a smiling rat on his brown forearm.

"I know."

"But you did it anyway. You don't mind looking like a sucker?"

"No."

"See that's your problem. You're a nice lady and people end up using you. Just sayin' that not everyone needs help. Sometimes they got to fall down so that they work hard like the rest of us."

He sounded like he'd come from a job fair lecture. She admired his concern if not his advice. "You're right about working hard, but not about being a sucker. What people do with a helping hand is none of my business."

"Yeah, but some people get more help than others."

Caryn nodded, it was getting personal and she didn't want to address this issue. "You're doing a great job. Keep it up and you'll go places, but get bitter and that will hold you down." She paid the amount quoted then took her purchases and left.

"I wanted to thank you again," the woman from the line said, meeting Caryn as she exited. "I can pay you back. It's just that my money hasn't been deposited yet and—"

"Don't worry," Caryn said, seeing the gray clouds coming in overhead and smelling the scent of rain. She hoped it would hold until she reached her car. "It's a gift."

"Not everyone would be so generous. You saved my day."

Caryn only smiled then noticed that the woman's cart brimmed with groceries and the child still slept undisturbed. "I'm no hero, just glad I could help."

"My name is Rita," she said, holding out her hand. "Rita Sanchez."

Caryn shook the woman's hand wondering why she felt the need to introduce herself. "Caryn Chandler."

"It's a true pleasure to meet you."

"Same, but I've got to dash."

A rumble of thunder drowned out her words, followed by the pounding sound of rain. As sleets of rain soaked the parking lot, Caryn sighed. She could make a run for it, but then she'd get drenched as would her items. She'd just have to wait it out. She noticed a small group of other shoppers deciding to do the same.

"Come," Rita said. "There's a bench over there."

Caryn briefly sent a look of longing to her car, then followed.

Once they were seated, Rita pulled out a little black

book and a white envelope fell out of her handbag. Caryn reached down and saw the word 'Groceries' spelled across it and felt the small stack of bills inside. She held the money out to her. "You dropped this."

Rita shook her head. "I wondered where that was. Keep it."

"But—"

"You can count it if you don't trust me."

"No, that's not it."

"Good then we're even." She opened the black book and grabbed a pen from her handbag. "But one good favor deserves another. What do you do?"

It was an odd question, but since the rain would fall for a few minutes, a chat would make time go by faster. "I'm a professional organizer."

Rita started to write then stopped and shook her pen. "Just when you need it most..." She shook the pen then tried writing with it again. It still wouldn't write. "This is why I wish I could do this on my cell phone," she mumbled to herself. "But rules are rules."

Caryn opened her handbag. "I may have a pen," she said not understanding why Rita would need it anyway.

"No, I'll get it to work." She dabbed the pen against her tongue before trying again. "See? That's better. Okay, what do you do again?"

"I don't see—"

"Just humor me."

"I'm a certified professional organizer also known as a CPO."

Rita scribbled something down, turning her body in a

way that Caryn couldn't see. "Ooh I love careers with acronyms. And how long have you been divorced?"

Caryn blinked surprised. "I'm not divorced. Why would you think that?"

"You just have the look of someone who's in an emotional state right now, as if you've lost something or someone that meant something to you."

I did. "I just have that kind of face."

"Are you in a relationship?"

"I don't discuss my private life." The woman was strange. Maybe she should risk getting wet. She stood. "I'd better go."

"Wait, I didn't mean to offend you, but I thought you deserved a chance."

"A chance?"

"What if you could turn your life, especially your love life, around? Would you talk about it then?"

Caryn paused then glanced at the still sleeping child, surprised that neither the rain nor the thunder had woken her. "That's impossible."

Rita shrugged. "Maybe. Isn't there anything you wished could be different?"

Yes, but doesn't everyone? Caryn thought, suddenly intrigued, rather than annoyed, by the woman. Her hawk- like features no longer seeming as pinched and harsh, her brown gaze sending her a silent message she couldn't quite interpret, but wanted to. "Not really."

"There's someone you love who could be yours if you really go for him."

Caryn sat down and stared at the rain. Its ferocity

hadn't ebbed. "He's in love with someone else," she said in a soft voice.

Rita smiled. "So there *is* someone?"

"No, yes." She shook her head amazed that she'd admitted her feelings to a stranger. "Definitely no."

Rita's knowing smile remained. "Which is it?"

"It's nothing. Unless you're offering me a chance to turn back time, then you can't help me."

"That's the mistake most people make. You don't need to change the past to change the future. By changing your present, you change your future."

"That sounds good, but I've done too many things wrong to change my future now. It's all set."

"Are you sure about that?"

"Yes."

"And what does your future look like?"

She'd never really thought about it. What did she want her future to look like? She wanted her business to continue to be successful. She wanted her family to be happy and she wanted her own wedding and a honeymoon and a wonderful marriage. Wait...where had that come from?

"There's nothing wrong with listening to your heart's desire."

Caryn wanted to joke and say how could she listen to anything with all this noise, but the sound of the rain and the sight of the gray clouds made her heart feel heavy and she felt ashamed. Ashamed that she'd dare to dream about something she'd run away from. "My heart is wrong. It's frivolous and silly."

"You only think that because you're afraid. I should know. I was the same way." She glanced away, her gaze settling on a woman carrying a large yellow, duck shaped umbrella and a boy in a raincoat and blue boots splashing in the puddles. "I was afraid of so many things, especially love."

"And then what happened?"

Rita closed her eyes. "Then I lost it all. My health, then my business, then some friends, and I realized what truly mattered in life."

"Love?"

"No, joy. We seek so many things, but all we really want to be is happy and joyous. I pretended for years to be what I thought I should be, even though I was miserable inside." She tapped her chest. "I won't say it was misery that caused my illness because that would make it too simplistic, but I will say it helped me to wake up. It helped me to see that I had only one life and I was wasting it. So I decided to change my future at that moment." She turned to Caryn. "And I'm asking you now, are you willing to make a change?"

Caryn bit her lip.

"It's okay to be afraid, but it's not okay to do nothing."

Caryn nodded. "Yes, I do want to change, but I have so many other things to do and I'm—"

Rita's face spread into a wide grin. "I'm glad to hear it. You're too young to settle into the routine you've created for yourself. You can't organize everything. Some things in life are a little messy and chaotic, but thrilling." She jotted some notes in her black book then said, "What kind of man do you want?"

A man I've already lost. "I don't know."

"That's okay." Rita snapped the black book closed then smiled. "Look, the rain's stopped."

Caryn turned, surprised to no longer hear the sound of rain, but instead the wheels of shopping carts, and car doors slamming shut. She looked up and saw patches of blue in the gray sky and watched as the sunbeams made the raindrops glitter on cars, poles, and the tips of grass. Within minutes, the sun would burn all the rain away and it wouldn't look as if it had rained at all. One moment could wipe away another. Caryn smiled feeling suddenly hopeful. She may have lost Adrian, but perhaps there was someone else out there waiting for her.

Caryn turned to thank Rita, but then saw that she, the cart full of groceries, and the sleeping child were gone.

CHAPTER SIX

"You're sulking."

Adrian let his fingers languidly sweep over the piano keys as he played a slow country song by memory. "I'm not sulking."

Roberta rested her hands on her hips and tilted her head. "You've hardly said a word to me."

He played a little louder. "There's nothing to say."

"She seemed as hesitant about taking this job as you are, but I convinced her to stay."

"How did you manage that? I couldn't."

"What?"

He increased the volume a little more, letting his fingers hit the keys with more force. "Never mind."

"She even offered to do it for free."

He gritted his teeth. "You'll pay her."

"I was going to, I just thought you'd want to know—"

"I don't want to know anything about her. Ever. If you're going to use her, don't tell me about it."

"You don't have to shout."

"I'm not shouting."

"Then stop playing so loud."

He changed to another song.

She rolled her eyes. "I hate when you play those tunes. You act like you were born in Tennessee instead of Delaware."

He chose a song that mingled country and hip hop then shot her a glance. "That better?"

She threw up her hands. "I wish you'd stop playing and listen to me."

"I'm listening."

"You're sulking. I thought you said you'd trust me to get you organized. I find one of the best organizers around and you respond like this just because you don't like her."

He switched to an R&B song.

"She will stay out of your way, you won't even notice her and it will all be done within a day or two. I'm doing this for your own good, so don't fight me on this, okay?"

He continued to play.

Roberta sighed then kissed him on the cheek. "Good." She left.

The moment she left, he stopped playing and slammed the piano lid close.

Eight years. Eight *years.* He was supposed to be completely over her by now. He wasn't supposed to feel anything. He was supposed to feel numb. He'd wiped Caryn from his mind. She didn't matter. Then why had he stood in the parking lot wanting to shake her? Wanting to force her to look at him and tell him why she'd hurt him? Why she'd run out on him?

But what was worse, was her mouth. She kept licking her lips and distracting him. She always did that when she was nervous. And the sight of her pink tongue sliding over her lush, full lips made him want to taste her. Feel her lips on his, pull her close and feel the soft give of her breasts against his chest. But it was her mouth that had always been the most dangerous to him. Seeing her again had been a shock, but he could barely focus on what she was saying, all he could think of was forcing her mouth to stop moving with one long, wet kiss. Those types of kisses used to be her favorite. "You can never kiss me enough," she used to say with a smile.

He preferred what the kissing led to—her legs wrapped around him, the soft brush of her breath against his skin as she sighed with pleasure.

Just one look at her again had stripped all the years away and his heart burst and bled as if he were still that twenty-seven year old groom jilted at the altar. If he hadn't been so broke, he would have left town, traveled for a year until he'd felt certain that he'd forgotten her. Unfortunately, he'd had nowhere to go, so he buried himself in the new food truck venture he and his friend Ken had devised. Deadly Delectable Pies, which sold pies by the slice. It wasn't an instant hit, but through diligence and consistency they gathered a devoted following. Soon they added a successful bakery, a restaurant and had invested in a food-delivery service. He wasn't broke anymore and in a city of more than a hundred thousand he'd believed it was unlikely he'd ever see her again.

Then there she was.

In the early days, he'd practiced what he'd say to her if they ever bumped into each other. He'd be cool and distant, hopefully have a hot girlfriend at his side and pretend to struggle to remember her name. And his wish had almost come true. He had a good looking girlfriend and money to throw around. He was an unmitigated success and he could flaunt it and show Caryn what she'd lost.

Instead he'd barely been able to speak. Why had she nearly killed herself sneaking out of his apartment? Why was she wearing a wig? Why wouldn't she look at him?

When he saw her limping, rage stirred up in him again. Because he cared. Why the hell did he still care? He wanted to lift her up in his arms and carry her to her car and check to make sure she was okay. He wanted to hold her close and feel the weight of her head on his shoulder. He wanted to be her hero.

And soon rage mingled with pain. That's what bothered him the most. She could still hurt him without doing anything. He hated that he'd let her capture his heart so completely and that he was still piecing back its remnants.

Adrian lifted the piano lid and began to play again. A calypso folk song "Yellow Bird" that his mother used to hum to him to get him to sleep. It always calmed him. And as he played he thought of her, her soft hands as she stroked his forehead, the smell of nutmeg that clung to her apron and he felt his pain fade. In his mind he heard her humming. He closed his eyes and soon heard singing, a clear beautiful voice. He remembered a soft caress on his cheek, and then he remembered Caryn singing the song too. She'd sung it to him when he'd been in bed recovering from the flu. And he remembered her singing it in harmony to a song on his stereo as she prepared a meal of curried rice and chicken.

Adrian opened his eyes, angered at the feel of stinging tears and pounded the keys with his fists. He. Was. Over. Her.

He shoved himself from the piano and stood. He wasn't going to go through this again. He was glad Roberta was forcing him to face this. He had to make himself not care. He didn't care that he could smell her scent linger on his couch...or was that just his imagination? He didn't care that he could see where she'd straightened a painting, or book or plant...or was that just from his memory?

The Caryn he'd seen was far from the woman he'd remembered. The beautiful bride who'd held his hand and looked up at him in tears and whispered, "I'm sorry. I can't."

"Please don't do this." He still hated himself for asking her to stay. He remembered grabbing her hand, feeling her shaking, seeing the tears in her eyes, feeling the gathering tears in his own. Then he remembered her turning and running out of his life.

No this Caryn was a faded memory of her former self. Adrian fell onto his couch and turned on the TV, eager to remember all her flaws. Roberta was definitely prettier and slimmer. Although Caryn had always been on the curvy side and he liked her round cheeks and puffy raspberry lips. No, he had to remember what he didn't like. He didn't like her clothes, but she'd never been stylish. Roberta matched him there. With her crooked wig Caryn had reminded him of a chipmunk. Although he'd always found chipmunks rather cute…

Adrian grabbed a pillow and screamed into it. Damn it! He didn't want to think of her as cute. She wasn't. She was just eight years older, wearing a wig for goodness sakes; dressed as if she were handing out pamphlets to save somebody's soul. He'd never fall for a woman like that again. Damn. What had made him fall for her in the first place? No, he wouldn't answer that. He knew why, but…He. Was. Over. Her.

He'd been angry, but he wasn't anymore. She wasn't a threat to him. If he ever saw her again, which he planned not to, he wouldn't be rattled. His life was good and she wouldn't be a part of it. She'd hurt his pride that was all. His heart was safe. Completely.

He hadn't felt anything when he'd seen her at the wedding. He still didn't know why he'd gone. He hated weddings. But Roberta had convinced him, as she usually did, and he'd enjoyed the ceremony and wished the couple well. He hadn't expected to see Caryn's sister there. What were the chances that she'd be the step-mother? Fortunately, there were enough people for him to stay out of view. He'd tried to convince Roberta to leave early, but she was determined to attend the reception.

They'd arrived early and he saw Caryn taking charge as usual. He overheard someone say that Caryn had saved them because the wedding planner had double booked. The irony wasn't lost on him. She saved one ceremony but couldn't stay for her own. He had no desire to see her again, but then saw her being accosted by a chubby little cherub and offered to help. He should have let the kid break her back.

He turned off the TV and grabbed a jump robe that he kept in the corner with some weights and began jumping.

He didn't want to admire her. He'd already made that mistake. He was smarter than that now. He increased his speed until the jump rope whistled as it sliced through the air as a blur.

He. Was. Over. Her.

And he continued to jump, bouncing like a spring, until sweat soaked his shirt; repeating his mantra, wanting it to be true.

Nearly an hour later, he stopped jumping and let the rope fall to the ground. His cell phone rang as he headed to the bedroom to shower. He glanced at the number and saw it was his friend and business partner, Ken.

"Yeah?"

"I'm at the restaurant."

Adrian couldn't help a smile. His friend was almost always at their new restaurant to make sure things were running according to his direction. "Is that supposed to surprise me?"

"I need you to come over quick."

"Why?"

"Because I'd like to give you the chance to do something before I kill somebody."

CHAPTER SEVEN

"You made the right decision," Barbara Lancaster said, setting her tea cup down on the accompanying saucer with a soft click.

She and Caryn sat in her aunt's island inspired kitchen nook where framed pictures of the two Bed and Breakfasts she owned hung on the walls. Caryn usually came up with excuses to avoid tea time with her aunt, but felt a little adrift after meeting Adrian and the strange conversation she'd had with Rita, the woman she'd met at the grocery store. Rita had her thinking about impossible things, but she knew her Aunt Barbara's no nonsense manner always grounded her in reality. Caryn's aunt, her mother's older sister of only eighteen months, although, at times, the distance seemed much greater, had a cool polished mahogany good looks, short black hair and a slender neck which boasted an intricate gold necklace from her late husband, who'd passed away three years ago. The simple gold band on her wedding finger sparkled as brilliantly as it had on her wedding day more than forty years ago.

"You were young," her aunt continued referring to Caryn's wavering feelings of regret, "and he didn't know where he was going in life. Your mother—"

"I know," Caryn said quickly, not wanting another reminder of how much her aunt had curbed her away from being anything like her mother. Not that she had to work hard. Caryn knew from a young age how much she didn't want to be like the pretty woman who'd given her her curvy figure and pouty mouth. A woman who didn't listen to anyone, who lived recklessly and on her own terms no matter who it hurt.

But at times, in the quiet, a voice whispered that she may have a little of her mother in her. That she had a wild nature that would at one point take over and destroy the carefully, controlled life she'd created. She'd come close to succumbing to her mother's wild ways when she'd agreed to marry Adrian after knowing him for less than five months. In him she felt as if she'd met her other half, the one who she wanted to spend her life with. But on her wedding day, the alarm bells rang. And as she stared up at Adrian on that day, fear gripped her: A fear that she loved him too much. She was afraid her love for him would consume her. And her mother had shown her what an all consuming love could do. The damage it could cause.

"I'm glad we agree," her aunt said with a soft smile. "I'm sure seeing him again was upsetting, but don't let him rattle you. He was being rash and impulsive when he convinced you of the insane idea, but what else is youth for?"

"It wasn't just his idea—"

"Now that you are both older, you must realize that the paths you've taken are for the best."

Caryn added more cream to her tea, pleased that her hand didn't shake, although she was trembling inside. She didn't feel older and more rational, not when it came to him. She felt young and giddy. Her skin still remembered the touch of his hand wrapped around her wrist, how it made all her senses come alight. She felt renewed again. A sense of anticipation, but for what? He always had that affect on her even in the past. He thrilled her, challenged her, forced her to expand beyond her rational safe ways without making her feel afraid. He'd dared her to be more, to dream of a life of adventure that they would share together. Would they have stayed together if she hadn't run away? What could have been?

"If you wanted milk, dear, you should have just told me."

Caryn looked down at her tea, which now nearly spilled over the brim, it's dark color now almost white. She set the creamer down. "I'm sorry."

"I understand. You're not yourself today."

"Do you really not have any regrets about him?"

Her aunt lifted her perfectly arched brows and rested a hand on her chest. "Me? Regrets about him? Why would I?"

"He offered you a chance to invest in his business."

"And he was totally unprofessional about it." Her aunt pursed her lips in disgust. "What a ludicrous idea.

Selling slices of pies from a food truck. He didn't even have a bakery first, that would have been a more reasonable start. Plus, why was he and his friend thinking of desserts when at the time they could have grabbed hold of a popular trend of Korean tacos? You'd think his friend would have at least thought to do that, considering his background."

"Ken isn't Korean, Aunty, and his specialties are desserts."

"Well, what sensible person waits until the last minute until the website is functional, dillydallies for days on the name and business structure, and tells an investor he and his partner has a backup plan in case things didn't work out?"

"He was being cautious."

"When I invest in something, I want the person to be truly committed without any doubts."

"But you could have been rich."

"I'm comfortable. I'm sure it was pure luck that propelled his business to the heights it's risen."

"Perhaps in the first year, but the last six took skill. Adrian's a savvy businessman and Ken knows it."

Her aunt shrugged. "I still don't regret it."

Caryn lifted her tea cup, making sure not to spill a drop, and took a long sip. "I wish I could say the same."

"You may not be as wealthy as he is, but you are very successful and—"

"Alone."

"Because the right man hasn't come along yet, but he will. Be patient." She clasped her hands together. "Actually—"

"No."

She frowned. "It's rude to interrupt."

Caryn took another sip of her tea then set the cup down. "I'm sorry Aunty, but the answer is still the same."

"You don't even know what I'm about to say."

"Leland Banks is single again and interested."

Barbara shrugged. "Okay, so you did know what I'm about to say."

"When I need an allergist, I'll look him up."

"He's a great catch."

"His name reminds me of an apartment complex."

Barbara made a tsking sound with her tongue. "Don't be petty."

"And he bores me."

"He's a little staid, but you could loosen him up."

"I don't want to."

"You're getting to the age," she paused and thoughtfully tapped her chin, "well actually *past* the age, where you can waste your time on useless men like Peter. I won't try to set you up, but I will tell you this, if you want to be truly happy you'll forget about Adrian Everett."

CHAPTER EIGHT

The moment he arrived in the kitchen of their Lucky Stars restaurant, Adrian knew why Ken was furious. The server was handling toast without wearing gloves, a whipped cream topped crepe sat neglected under a warmer, the lunch tray set up was all wrong, and salt and pepper shakers had gone missing. But the worst was when he spotted a cook overdoing the eggs at one of the griddles.

In his early days, Ken would have yelled, taken the griddle and thrown the eggs against the wall and humiliated the cook, but Adrian had helped him cool his temper, and when he didn't think he could, he called him in.

"I don't want you to speak," Adrian calmly said, taking over the cook's position. "I just want you to watch." He dumped the eggs in the trash then started again, quickly showing the younger man how to produce soft eggs. Once he was finished, he patted the man on the back and said, "I know you can do better. Now show me."

He then efficiently dealt with the other mistakes, helping to locate the missing salt and pepper shakers, gently reminding the server the importance of wearing gloves and why it was part of their culture, repeating the proper procedure for the warmer and showing them how the lunch tray was to be set.

After the mini crisis had been settled, he found Ken pacing in the back alley behind the restaurant, where puddles of rain reflected the blue sky above. He wore dark jeans and a crumpled white shirt, and ran a hand through his bed head spiked black hair.

"You fixed things?" Ken asked, his Portuguese accent only lightly touching the edge of his words. "Disaster, it has been avoided?"

Adrian smiled. "That's why I'm paid the big bucks."

"That server—"

"I know. I took care of it all, but I have to give you credit. I'm surprised you waited for me to handle the guy with the eggs."

Ken paused, his gaze sharpening. "What guy? What eggs?"

Adrian silently swore. Either Ken hadn't seen it or had left the kitchen before he could see. "It's nothing."

He kicked a dumpster, startling some pigeons who flew from a ledge. "Some guy can't even cook a f--- egg!"

"He can now."

"Did you fire him?"

"You know I didn't come here to do that."

"Tell me who it is. The guy with the peach fuzz on his lip? I promise I won't touch him."

"No."

"I won't shout. I won't even raise my voice."

Adrian rested a hand on Ken's tense shoulder. For years he'd always been Ken's good manners and knew how to soothe him. Ken had the brilliant ideas; Adrian made them work. Although they'd both attended New York's French Culinary Institute, they'd met at one of Ken's small restaurants, one that eventually closed due to mismanagement and creative differences with his then partner, a man who Ken made cry on numerous occasions.

When Adrian was hired as a food-safety consultant, Ken immediately saw Adrian's other talents, and the pair came up with the plan for Deadly Delectable Pies. Ken didn't care that Adrian's previous business, a startup company that created collapsible high heel shoes, flopped. Their different personalities blended well. Initially, Adrian had to get past Ken's volatile reputation as the 'crazy Asian guy with the Spanish accent', which really ticked Ken off. *"I'm not Spanish,"* he'd say before smashing something. Adrian had to work hard before he could get investors interested. But he did and through effort and strategy they created a baked goods chain with six locations and other lucrative ventures.

"Relax," Adrian said, giving Ken's shoulder a squeeze. "You don't have to worry anymore. The eggs will be so fluffy and soft they'll float out of the kitchen."

Ken ran his hand through his hair again, looking like

a man in need of a cigarette or a stiff drink. "You're sure everything is fine?"

"Yes," Adrian said, folding his arms, sensing his friend's bad mood was lifting. "I took care of things. It's all right now."

"If everything's all right, why do you look like hell?"

Adrian blew him a kiss. "I love you too."

Ken's brows drew together. "What's going on?"

I saw Caryn again. "Roberta's organizing my place."

Ken snapped his fingers and pointed him."*Péssima ideia,* didn't I tell you that?"

Adrian scratched his cheek. "I needed to do something about the bears. When I said I'd help my sister I didn't think it would get out of hand."

"Are we talking about the same sister? The one who in college offered a cartoon drawing to anyone who signed up for her mailing list and ended up getting eight hundred responses?"

"I know, she didn't think the donations would come so fast or be so many."

Ken stared at him for a long moment. "You're sure that's all it is?"

Adrian glanced to his right then his left. "Has this alley turned into a confessional or something?"

Ken softly swore and hung his head. "You're doing it."

Adrian held out his hands in a helpless gesture. "Doing what?"

He looked at him. "Making things light. You always do that when things are bad. Is it you and Roberta?"

"You still don't like her?"

Ken couldn't help a smile. "Are you thinking of cutting her loose?"

"No."

"Then what is it?"

"The bears. I'm having nightmares about the bears. That's all."

Ken nodded. "Fine, you had me worried." He hit him on the arm. "Come on, let's get a drink," he said, heading down the alley. "I'm glad that's all it is."

"Why?"

"Because you looked like you'd just seen a ghost."

CHAPTER NINE

Forget Adrian Everett. If only she could. She desperately wanted to. Caryn drove home annoyed by her traitorous heart and mind. He was taken. It was over. She didn't have a chance. She didn't want a chance. They were too different and they'd met purely by accident at Terri's Halloween party eight years ago…

"Why didn't you come together?" Terri asked, adjusting the hat of her Red Crayola crayon costume when she saw Caryn searching the crowd of goblins, fake celebrities, witches and warlocks for her date, Philip.

"He has a late shift at work."

"What's he supposed to be?"

Caryn tugged on her long blonde wig then gestured to her red Renaissance maiden costume. "I'm Princess Buttercup."

"Who?"

"The princess from the movie *The Princess Bride* and he's going to be—"

Terri held up her hand. "Let me guess...Inigo Montoya."

"No," Caryn said, making a face. "My true love Westley as the Dread Pirate Roberts."

Terri nodded to a man dressed in black, like a pirate, getting a drink at the punch bowl. "Then I think I see him."

Caryn's heart jumped to her throat, fear that he wouldn't show slipping away replaced by joy. "Yes, that's him!"

Terri pushed her forward then waved. "Have fun storming the castle!"

Caryn rushed over to the table, spun him around and kissed him, barely reaching his mouth since he was a lot taller than she remembered. She took a step back and grinned up at him. He looked like a true darkly, handsome raider of the sea in a pirate headscarf mask, swashbuckler shirt, boot tops with wide cuffs at the knee and lace-up details. She never imagined Philip would go to such lengths since he'd seemed reluctant to attend the party.

"You look amazing," Caryn said in awe. "This costume is great." She playfully squeezed his forearm, surprised by how well he filled his shirt. "Is this padding?" she said with a giggle.

"Um...I think..."

She held up her hands not wanting him to feel awkward. "I know. You thought it was silly of me to be a black princess with blonde hair, but I just wanted to have fun. And at least we match." She took his hand again surprised by how large and warm it felt. Maybe because she was seeing him in a new way she was responding to him differently too. Usually his hands were cold and dry. "I want to show you something."

She took him outside to the balcony where Terri had trimmed the black railing with orange and white lights, above them the moon hung low in the inky black sky. She turned to him ready to thank him, but she didn't get the chance. His mouth covered hers, his lips more persuasive than she'd ever remembered them to be. He felt wonderful, better than he ever had before, and as his arms wrapped around her midriff she felt as if she were in a true fairytale and she whispered, "I want to be with you forever."

And he said in a husky whisper, "As you wish."

She drew away and stared at him in wonder, feeling as if she were under a spell. "I've never felt this way before."

"Neither have I."

Even his voice sounded a little different. She took his hand. "You're shaking."

"Yes, because there's something you should know."

"Caryn!" a familiar male voice said.

She spun around and saw a prince instead of a pirate. A man who looked like Cinderella's Prince Charming dressed in a white military style jacket with a gold sash. A prince who didn't wear a black mask, who knew her name and sounded just like Philip. "Terri said I'd find you out here."

"Philip?" she said, just to make sure.

"Sure," he said with a laugh. "Who else would I be?"

Oh no. Oh no. She slowly turned to the man next to

her. The beautiful, sexy pirate who she'd kissed with abandon. "I owe you an apology."

He held her hand, his gaze intense. "No, don't run from this," he said in a velvet whisper.

"What's going on?" Philip asked.

The stranger continued to hold her gaze. "We fell in love."

She swallowed. That was crazy. She couldn't have fallen in love with someone she'd just met based on a kiss. Then why did it feel so right? Why did she feel as if she'd found what she'd always been looking for?

"Caryn?" Philip asked. "What is he talking about?"

She took a hasty step back, pulling her hand free, but unable to break his gaze. "I don't know."

"Do you know the café on Fenton Street?" the pirate-stranger asked.

"Yes," she said feeling breathless, wondering why he still had this hold on her without touching her.

"If you feel what I do, meet me there tomorrow at three." He nodded then left.

Philip watched him go. "Who the hell was that?"

"I don't know," Caryn said, watching her pirate disappear into the crowd.

"YOU HAVE to go and see him," Terri said after the party had ended. Caryn helped her clean up the empty plates and cups and take down the decorations.

Caryn picked up some paper plates and dumped

them in her trash bag. "You mean you don't know who it could be?"

Terri removed a string of orange ribbon from a lamp. "No, and I wouldn't tell you if I did."

"Why not?"

"Because I want you to go and find out more about him."

"How could I when I embarrassed myself?"

"He didn't seem to mind. You're curious, and we both know you're not that serious about Philip. At least see if there could be something with him or if tonight was just a little Halloween magic."

THE MAGIC SEEMED to have faded as Caryn sat in the crowded café waiting for the stranger to appear. It was three o'clock exactly and he was nowhere in sight. She waited ten more minutes then came to the conclusion that he'd made a fool of her. She left the café and was half way to her car when she heard someone cry out "Wait!"

She turned and saw a man coming towards her on a bicycle. He braked, jumped off his bicycle and hopped over to her as if he were in pain. Before she could ask any questions he ripped off his helmet and flashed her a heart melting grin. "You came. I wasn't sure you would."

"Yes," was all that she could manage, surprised that her presence could cause such joy on his face. Without the black headscarf mask, she saw he was even better looking than she'd imagined, and when a burst of wind sent leaves of gold, ruby, and amber swirling around them, she felt as if the magic of last night had settled around them once more.

"I'm sorry I'm late," he said, gripping the handles of his bicycle. It was then that she noticed how tight his knuckles were. She dropped her gaze further and saw blood on his sneakers and a large gash on his leg.

Her mouth fell open. "What is wrong with you!"

The light in his eyes dimmed. "What?"

"You're hurt."

A flash of chagrin touched his face. "Yeah, a minor accident getting here. Mind if I rest against your car a minute?"

"You need to go to the hospital." She knelt down and looked closer at the wound. "Looks very bad." She glanced up at him. "Does it hurt?"

"It feels like it's on fire and being attacked by wasps at the same time, but other than that I'm fine."

She stood. "I'll take you to the hospital." She pointed at him. "And don't say no."

More than three hours later, she was driving him home, after he'd received stitches and a prescription for painkillers. But in those three hours she'd learned his name, learned that he'd gotten hit by a car on his way to see her, that he could joke even in pain, and that he was just as wonderful as when she'd met him the night before. She learned that he could be impulsive, and that she liked him immensely, maybe even loved him. Although she didn't believe in love at first sight, he made her wonder.

"You could have cancelled," she chided him as she drove him back to his place.

He rested his head back and closed his eyes. "I didn't have your phone number."

"You could have gotten it from Terri."

"Who?"

"The woman who hosted the Halloween party."

He nodded but didn't open his eyes. "Oh right."

"And then you could have told her that you need to tell me something." Caryn glanced at him. "And I know you're going to say that you didn't know my name, but you could have told her that I was the one in the blonde wig dressed like Princess Buttercup and then she would have known who you were talking about and relayed the message to me."

A slow smile spread on his lips. "What fun would that be?"

She glanced at his bandaged leg. "You call this fun?"

He shot her a look of mischievous pleasure. "I got to spend time with you, didn't I?"

Caryn pulled her gaze away and stared at the road. "It was still dangerous. You could have gotten an infection and—"

He reached over and tenderly stroked her cheek. "I'm glad you came," he said in a soft voice.

She bit her lip, knowing she should pull away from such a bold caress, her skin tingling from his touch, as if he were a magician casting a spell. Instead she reached out her hand to him, feeling a sigh of relief when she felt his warm hand close over hers. "This is crazy," she said.

"I know, but don't fight it."

"We hardly know each other."

He grinned. "It won't take long to change that."

"I'm not sleeping with you on the first date."

He laughed. "That's not what I meant."

She felt her face color. "Oh."

"But I look forward to that too." He squeezed her hand. "A lot." He kissed the back of her hand. "So much." He kissed her palm. "I don't think I'll be able to sleep tonight just thinking about it," he said, licking her palm with the tip of his tongue.

She yanked her hand away, her face no longer burning from embarrassment, and playfully slapped him on the arm. "Cut that out."

He rubbed his arm, feigning hurt. "You'd strike a wounded man?"

"Yes, because he's dangerous."

"You're right," he said without remorse then studied his nails. "Well, a pirate is known to steal." He sent her a look. "And your heart is high on my list."

By the end of the day he had her heart completely and barely five months later she was eager to be his bride. But it was as she stood in front of him at the altar, her heart full of love, that her dream shattered as she stared at her greatest secret sitting in the crowd. A secret that would destroy everything.

A secret that wasn't new and one that wouldn't go away.

Her life had been all about secrets. She'd never invited friends over to her house, there had been no sleep-overs, birthday parties, having friends over to hang out or to study. She kept everyone away so that no one could find out that she was living in misery.

Caryn didn't want anyone to discover that she

didn't know whether their house had carpeting or hard-wood flooring, because it was buried under two feet of trash. Trash her mother called her 'darling treasures.' Her mother went shopping every weekend and filled the house with more and more stuff, but it wasn't just the items she purchased. She kept the wrapping paper from any gifts they received, the boxes the items came in, the receipts, the extra buttons that came with shirts and jackets, she reused paper towels and still had extra rolls.

Some items were stacked so high that they covered the windows and threatened to touch the ceiling.

And if Caryn tried to clean anything—if she moved a toothbrush, one of fifty, or touched an empty box of Kleenex—somehow her mother knew and had a fit. She never hit her, but her words were just as effective, scar-ring her heart and making her flinch like a physical assault.

Caryn kept her secret from teachers, other family members, and child protection services, because as much as she wanted to leave, she knew her mother needed her. She kept the secret from her brother who went to live with their father. Her mother holding on to her saying "I'm so glad you won't abandon me like everyone else."

And when her mother hugged her in those moments she felt guilty for wanting to leave her, wanting to disap-pear and be somewhere clean.

She wanted to be in a place where she didn't have stacks of clothing on the floor and on the bed. Her mother always buying her more, even though she'd told her she didn't need them.

She once said they had a problem, mentioned the word 'hoarder' but her mother had bristled at the term.

"Those are filthy people," she'd said. "I'm just a collector and creative."

Her mother was blind to it all. And every day Caryn felt as if she were suffocating. It was when her younger sister started to take on some of their mother's habits that she made a decision to reach out to their father to take her too.

She didn't give him a reason, just that she was doing poorly in school, which was true, and that mother wasn't patient with her, also true. Fortunately, her mother let Ella go not caring as long as she had Caryn.

Then when Caryn was seventeen, her Uncle Murray got sick and her Aunt Barbara wasn't coping well. Caryn offered to help and saw a way out. She cared for him for six months until he recovered then the thought of returning to her mother's house caused her to break down. Her aunt found Caryn in the shower fully clothed, crouched with her knees to her chest mumbling to herself. "I can't go back. I can't go back."

With patience and tenderness she'd gotten Caryn out of the shower.

"Now tell me what's wrong."

"I can't."

"Yes, you can."

"You'll have to see it or you won't believe me."

"See what?"

"The house, but you'll have to wait until she's at work or she won't let you."

The look of horror on her aunt's face when they

entered her house the next day, confirmed all her fears. It truly was hell. It was as bad as she remembered it.

"Pack your things," she said in a brisk voice. "You're not coming back here."

"There's nothing I want. Please let's go."

"Dear God," her aunt said, squeezing her way through a tunnel of boxes and crawling over a mound of clothes, towels and paper. She finally reached the front door and said, "This is absolutely abominable." She swung it open, stumbled outside then fanned herself as if she were about to faint. "Why didn't you tell anyone?"

Caryn closed the front door and locked it. "I was afraid of what would happen to us. To her."

Barbara took a step back and stared up at the house and its pristine green shutters and tended garden of purple azalea bushes and pink peonies. "You couldn't tell from the outside how bad it is." She brushed away the remnants of a spider's web that clung to the sleeve of her jacket. "I never saw anything like this when we were growing up. She needs help."

She doesn't want help. I've tried. But Caryn didn't tell her aunt this, instead she balled her hands into fists and quietly said, "Can I stay with you? I won't be any trouble and—"

Barbara turned to the car and waved the rest of Caryn's words aside. "You don't need to convince me, dear, you're never coming back here."

And she didn't. Her aunt kept her word despite the battle her mother initially raged against her, leaving foul phone messages, texts and emails. But when Barbara threatened to report her to the county, she quieted down and left Caryn alone, although it was years before she spoke to her again.

During their separation, Caryn depended on her Aunt Barbara to show her how to live a life out in the open without secrets and insanity. Caryn modeled her aunt's every action wanting to be as professional and emotionally healthy as she was. Deep down, at times, she feared she had some of her mother's tendencies, she feared that she had something inside her that could snap and spin her life out of control as her mother's had. Her mother hadn't always been that way. For the first thirty-five years of her life she'd been 'normal'. Then came the separation and divorce, and a health crisis and that sent her over an edge she'd never returned from.

Her aunt had given Caryn stability and warned her against her mother's impulsiveness. "Your parents never should have married," her aunt told her one day during her brother's college graduation.

Her parents, who were both in attendance, pretended not to see each other, although her mother couldn't be missed in a light orange dress and matching shoes. No one could guess that she had seventy dresses just like it in different colors. "They were too young and it happened too fast. Your mother made your father her world and look where that left her. Don't let your life ever be ruled by your heart. It will only lead to heartbreak and ruin."

It was those words that flashed through her mind on her wedding day. She'd glanced at her mother smiling up at her, feeling the strength of her feelings for Adrian and knew that if she lost him it would destroy her. She felt like a fraud, as if she'd tricked him to falling into something that wasn't real. Her father had loved her mother once, but then her strange behavior had started after the birth of her sister. Adrian had never seen her mother's house; he didn't know what she could become, so she ran...

Caryn pushed the memory aside as she parked her car and briefly rested her head on the steering wheel. *You made the right decision*, her aunt had said. But her heart continued to rebel. She left her car, grabbed her mail then walked up to her townhouse determined to push her feelings away. She'd protected them both. She'd done the rational thing. She had used her head instead of her heart. He was better off without her and there was no turning back.

She walked into her foyer, placing her keys and handbag in their designated slots, before going through her mail. She flipped through the various sized envelopes with little interest, until one particular envelope caught her eye.

CHAPTER TEN

————————

Caryn set the other envelopes aside, sat on her couch and stared at it. It looked like a wedding invitation, but she'd never seen anything like it.

She checked the address and saw her full name: Caryn Angela Chandler. Who could it be from? She grabbed a letter opener and swiftly cut open the gold lined envelope. Inside was a handwritten note on expensive parchment paper lined with finely woven lace. *You have been personally selected to join The Black Stockings Society, an elite, members-only club that will change your life and help you find the man of your dreams. Guaranteed.*

Guaranteed? She rolled her eyes and grimaced. There were few guarantees in life. Someone had created an expensive form of junk mail. She wouldn't fall for it, but that didn't stop her from being curious. She read the rest of the note.

Dumped? No, she'd broken up with Peter.

Bored? Yes, she felt as if her life had hit a rut.

Tired of being single? She hadn't been single long—a week, maybe?—but would like to be in a relationship.

Ready to live dangerously?

She paused. She'd never lived dangerously. She always weighed her options and the consequences of her actions. That's why she'd let Adrian go. Agreeing to marry him after such a short time had been reckless. She shouldn't have even made it to the wedding. She shouldn't have allowed it to get that far. She shouldn't have hurt Adrian like that. Being reckless only hurt others in the long run, as her aunt constantly reminded her. Hadn't her mother taught her that? She'd had a whirlwind romance with her father.

But still...there was something that burned within her. She wanted more out of life. She wanted to feel that magic she'd felt when she'd spotted a sexy pirate from across the room. Caryn shook her head. But that was nonsense. She wasn't in her twenties anymore and that moment wasn't real, although everything about it had felt real. More real than anything in her life had felt before or since. Her love for Adrian had been real. She didn't want to love that completely again, but she didn't want to stay safe either. Could there be a healthy in-between? She read the sentence again.

Ready to live dangerously? She licked her lip, nodded her head then whispered 'yes.'

Then this is the club for you. Guaranteed results! Submit your application today.

Application? Why did she have to fill out an application? If she'd been invited didn't that mean she was chosen? What if she failed the application? Why would they get someone's hopes up like this? She flipped the card over, but couldn't find any more information. The Black Stockings Society? What exactly was it?

She decided to do a search, but couldn't find any information about them either online or off, which made her more curious instead of suspicious. How was she selected? What did a membership mean? Why didn't they have an email address, special website or at least a phone number where she could call and ask questions? She looked at the nominal fee that she was supposed to send with her application. The amount wasn't a lot of money, but why should she pay anything?

She set the paper aside three times and picked it up each time. She should throw it away, but twice she'd walked to her trash bin and couldn't let it go. She even made the motion of throwing it away, but it remained gripped in her hand. For a moment she felt like her mother, who kept every holiday card, unable to toss them in the recycling bin.

"I'm not her," Caryn said through gritted teeth, using one hand to tug the envelope out of the other's grip. But the hand seemed to have a mind of it's own and wouldn't let go.

She released a cry of frustration, fell to her knees then said, "Okay, just this once. I won't throw it away, that doesn't mean I'm losing it."

The other hand's tension relaxed and she felt herself

becoming at ease. Curiosity wasn't the same as recklessness. She was very aware of her every action. This wasn't an emotional choice, but one of intellectual intrigue.

Feeling more in control, Caryn got a pen, returned to the couch and looked at the enclosed questionnaire. Unfortunately, it didn't make sense to her. The questions were outrageous. She'd expected them to ask about her career or ambitions, perhaps a psychological test to make sure she was a prime candidate. Instead they seemed to focus on vague interests. She sighed. She'd come this far and there weren't many questions anyway so she might as well continue. She reread the first question.

Piano or guitar? Does it really matter? Were they trying to distinguish whether she preferred a string instrument or something? Did that say something about her personality? She skipped to the next question.

Rock climbing or white water rafting? She hadn't even considered either. Both were dangerous. Did she really have to chose? Would it matter if she didn't answer? Or perhaps she could make her own suggestion? She skipped to another question.

Winter or summer wedding? She gripped her pen. It should have been a simple question but it wasn't. Why did they have to ask her about a wedding? And why did they have to ask winter or summer instead of spring or fall? Her first time had been in the spring because she loved the season of new beginnings and the lighter days. Maybe this time it should be different. She wrote down winter.

Then she crossed it out and said summer. It was just

for fun, she might as well state what she really wanted—a day with bright sunshine and everything lush and green— even though it wasn't likely to come true.

She glanced back at the previous questions and quickly jotted down 'piano' and 'rock climbing' then jumped to the final question.

What is your ideal man like? She wrote down, I don't know. Then remembered Rita's question, 'What would you do if you could change your future?' She would like a second chance with Adrian. *You still love him.* But that was wrong. He was with someone else. She crossed off her words. If she really cared about him, she'd want him to be happy and Roberta seemed nice, a little bossy and pushy, but people at times said the same about her. So she wrote, I want to fall madly in love without going crazy. Is that even possible? I don't know, but I want a man who wouldn't be destroyed by my secrets. Who will forgive me my flaws and not run away from them and...

She tossed her pen down and sat back. She was asking too much and her reply didn't make sense. She wasn't being clear and precise. That's what a rational mind did. She was being emotional and bleeding on the page. She grabbed the application and began to crumple it up then stopped.

Don't run from this Caryn, it may be your only chance. She didn't know where the voice came from, but it sounded hurt and she heeded it's warning. She smoothed the application then quickly wrote, 'I don't want an ideal, I want my true love'.

Before she could change her mind she quickly read over the 'sworn' oath. *As a member of The Black Stock-*

ings Society, I swear I will not reveal club secrets, I will accept nothing but the best and I will no longer settle for less, signed the application, paid the nominal membership fee, using her credit card, and ran outside and popped it in the mailbox.

A COUPLE OF DAYS LATER, Caryn found a medium sized package in her mailbox. Inside the box, encased in a purple satin cloth, were four pairs of different types of stockings, a membership card that read *Caryn Angela Chandler, Member, The Black Stockings Society.*

She'd made it? She'd actually passed? They'd accepted her application and all her ramblings? Caryn danced around her apartment, pumping her fists and making up a few dance movements before returning to the package.

Welcome to The Black Stockings Society. Your first assignment is to take your membership card to Haven Spa, where you will receive the platinum plus. Your appointment for the platinum plus has already been reserved please arrive at this time.

Caryn saw the date and felt her stomach shrivel. She licked her lips. This can't be right. The appointment was set for today. She glanced at the clock. In less than two hours! Why hadn't they consulted her? How could they make a reservation without telling her? What if she didn't have her schedule free? What if she hadn't opened the package until later this evening? What if...?

But you did open it and your schedule is free, a

nagging voice said. *You wanted to live a little dangerously, so go for it.*

Caryn grabbed her keys and handbag and raced out the door.

CHAPTER ELEVEN

She'd never get away with this, Caryn thought looking at the exclusive address and exquisitely designed building. The application fee wasn't even close to what a simple wash and curl would cost at this place. Was someone playing a joke on her? She grabbed the silver door handle and pulled. She wouldn't know until she found out. She took a deep breath and walked up to the sleek black counter.

"My name is Caryn Chandler and I have an appointment for the platinum plus," she said smoothly, having practiced the line many times on her drive to the spa.

The clerk, a young woman with spiky black hair and porcelain skin, checked her computer. "I'm afraid you're not in the system. Are you sure it was for today?"

Could she have gotten the day wrong? Of course they wouldn't schedule something like this on the same day she received the package. In her excitement she must have gotten the date and time mixed up. Or maybe she'd gotten the location wrong. Caryn hastily pulled out her instructions. Her membership card slipped out and landed on the counter.

The clerk jumped up as if a frog had leapt out of Caryn's handbag. "Oh my God! Can I touch it?"

Caryn frowned. "Touch what?"

The clerk pointed at the card. "That."

"Sure," Caryn said not understanding the young woman's enthusiasm.

The woman swept it up as if it were a golden ticket. "I heard about this, but never seen one." She chewed her lower lip, a tinge of red touching her cheeks. "Please don't tell anyone I screwed up," she said, handing the card back to Caryn.

"But you haven't."

"I—"

Another woman about Caryn's age, but better dressed and a foot taller, approached them. "What's going on here?"

"There's a mistake regarding my appointment," Caryn said.

The young clerk looked sheepish, the tinge of red growing a deeper shade. "I'm sorry. I didn't see the card."

"It's probably my fault," Caryn said not wanting the young clerk to be reprimanded. "I didn't show it to her. Does it make a difference?"

The older woman sat down behind the computer. "More than you know." She looked at the screen. "Yes, your appointment is set. Please enjoy," she said, motioning to the hall.

"Thank you," Caryn said then paused. "Excuse me, but how is payment—"

"Your membership covers all costs. Enjoy."

Caryn nodded, turned and jumped when she saw a woman with intricate braids and silver eye shadow, standing behind her as if she'd appeared out of thin air.

"Please follow me," the woman said.

Moments later, Caryn found herself in a private suite wearing a green terry robe. She was treated to fresh strawberries dipped in chocolate and champagne, had a chocolate body wrap and massage, and a skin treatment. Then she was led into a room with a vanity and chair and seated. Within minutes three women entered and circled her chair.

"This is going to be interesting," the first woman, a full figured woman of Asian heritage with bright red lips, reddish brown hair, and sparkles on her lashes said, pressing her palms together as if in prayer.

The second woman narrowed her hazel gaze, folding twig-thin brown arms. "Are you sure she's a platinum plus client?" she said giving Caryn the once over.

"Yes," the third woman said, using a heavily ringed hand to touch the tips of Caryn's wig.

"My name is Lin," the first woman said with a smile.

"It's really Regina," the second woman said in a stage whisper. "But she wants to be exotic."

Lin shot her a look. "No, I just think the name suits me better."

"I'm Andrea," the second woman said. She motioned to the third woman. "And this is Patty. We're going to give you a total makeover. You'll leave here with new clothes—"

"And we'll redo your hair and makeup," Lin said.

"Well," Caryn said, glancing up. "This isn't my hair. I—"

Patty made an impatient motion with her hand. "You don't need to tell us. You weren't fooling anyone." She pulled the wig off and tossed it over her shoulder, expertly hitting the trash bin behind her. "That's the past." She looked at the other women. "Ladies, let's get to work."

Hours later, Caryn stared at herself in the full-length mirror, unable to believe her own eyes. They'd given her a stylish shoulder length black brown weave, redone her eyes to accentuate the gold highlights, chosen a deep purple hue for her lips, and dressed her in a black A line skirt and flirty red top. She looked ten years younger and felt like a new woman.

"Is this really me?" she said, stepping closer to the mirror and touching her hair.

"Yes," Patty said.

"The rest of your wardrobe will arrive tomorrow," Lin added.

Caryn turned to her, amazed. "You mean I get more?"

Andrea winked. "Girl, this is just the beginning."

AND AS PROMISED, a host of clothes arrived the next day, and Caryn stared at her newly filled closet, stunned.

At first she panicked a little. She'd never completely filled anything before—from notebooks to the cabinets in her kitchen—and didn't want too much. But fortunately, everything fit perfectly so her anxiety left her. She pinched herself then winced. Yes, this was real. She pulled out The Black Stockings Society package, which she'd hidden underneath the bed, and read the next instructions.

Once you have gone to the spa you will select and wear one of your stockings to your next client meeting.

Caryn laid out the four choices of stockings on the bed, and licked her lips, worried. None looked appropriate for a client meeting. For dancing or a night club scene? Yes. But in the daytime they seemed a little risqué. She slid on a pair of dark green fishnets, the feel of them like a second skin, and she felt an unfamiliar sensation come over her. A bold sensual power. Adrian's face flashed in her mind and suddenly she felt her body aching for the touch of his hand, the feel of his skin. An almost painful desire to be his woman again.

She stripped off the stockings and tossed them on the bed in horror. She stared at them as if they could leap up and attack her. What was going on? That was impossible. The whole request was crazy. How could she wear something like this to a client meeting? She lifted up the stockings holding them between her thumb and forefinger. She'd never worn something like that before. They made her feel like a different woman. She didn't like the feeling. They made her feel reckless and wild. She released them, folded her arms and looked at the other selections. None seemed appropriate.

Caryn fell on the bed, rubbing her forehead unsure what to do next. This was just the beginning of being a member of the club. She wanted to follow the instructions...but this was too much. However, if she wore a long skirt, no one would notice. She rushed to her closet and realized that the longest skirt reached just below her knees. Then again, she didn't have to wear a skirt, she could wear trousers. They didn't say she had to wear them with a skirt. Feeling more confident, she put her outfit together.

ROBERTA COULD HARDLY KEEP her mouth closed when Caryn arrived.

"What happened to you?" Roberta said, making a circle around Caryn.

"Just thought I'd try a new look."

"You should have tried it sooner." She held up a hand. "Not that I'm being rude or anything. It's just that I hardly recognized you."

"Thanks, but I'm not here for me. Let's get this place organized."

Although Roberta continued to gawk and stare, Caryn stayed professional. She looked over the homework she'd given to Roberta, surprised Adrian had even completed it, then she and her two assistants were able to organize the areas within hours.

As she watched everything being put into new drawers, closets and wire baskets, Caryn felt as if everything was moving in slow motion. She didn't realize how hard it would be to be in his place a third time. Her traitorous mind briefly flashing to his bedroom, ruminating on how his sheets would feel against her skin, how he'd feel when there were no sheets to separate them. She rubbed her hands against her trouser legs, a part of her wanting to give Roberta a peek of her stockings, just to say "You don't know me as well as you think you do. Adrian could fall for me again." But she managed to keep her cool. She was sensible, not flirty and definitely not seductive, although the stockings made her feel as if she could be. She'd take them off the moment she got home.

Once the project was completed, Roberta again looked around speechless. "You truly are a master. Adrian will love it."

"It was a pleasure working with you." *And I hope to never see you again.*

"Likewise. I'll keep your card in case my place needs you."

Damn. "That would be great."

Caryn returned home feeling as if a giant weight had been lifted off her shoulders. She'd survived without making a fool of herself. But as she approached her front door she saw an attractive, full figured, dark skinned woman leaning against it, wearing a blue silk dress and dangling silver earrings. She sent Caryn a fierce look. "Do you think you can get away with cheating?"

CHAPTER TWELVE

"Isn't it amazing! I told you she was the best, didn't I?"

Adrian sat behind his piano and flexed his fingers. "Hmm."

Roberta wrapped her arms around Adrian's neck and placed a noisy kiss on his cheek. "Don't you think she did a great job?"

He began to play a classic country song. "Sure."

"You hardly looked."

"I saw enough." He didn't want to admit that he had been impressed, that he wanted to open all the windows to rid his place of Caryn's scent because it still turned him on. She'd even left a workable plan for Monica's organization, giving his sister key contacts to help her implement a more sustainable and efficient plan to store and distribute the teddy bears. For that alone, he was in danger of falling in love with Caryn all over again. His place was now almost teddy bear free, and if he didn't see another button-eyed, fuzzy brown toy, it would be too soon.

Roberta sat on the piano bench beside him. "Well, if you think she's done anything to this place, you should have seen what she did to herself. She must have fallen in love or something."

Adrian's fingers fumbled over the keys, but he quickly corrected himself. "I don't want to talk about her."

"I was just so shocked. I didn't think a person could look so different."

"That's enough, Roberta."

"She didn't look like herself at all. She's had a complete makeover and it looked expensive."

"I said that's enough."

"I wonder where she got her hair done and...must you play that so loud?"

He didn't adjust his playing. "No."

"You play so well, you'd think you'd have better taste."

"I like country."

"I know," she said with a groan. "I'll get used to it when I move in."

Adrian stopped playing and stared at her. "What?"

Roberta gestured to the newly organized room. "You didn't think I was doing all this just for you, did you?"

He blinked. "Yes, I did."

"You may want to take your time, but I don't. It's time we moved in together. You want it as much as I do. You wouldn't have given me the keys to your place otherwise."

"I gave you the keys because—"

"You wanted me to take charge of getting your place organized," she said with a grin as if she knew something that he didn't. "That's your excuse, but your real reason is that you wanted to take our relationship to the next level."

"No, I—"

"We make such a great couple. All my friends think so."

"Roberta—"

"And my mother's already hearing wedding bells, but I told her that's down the road."

"Roberta—"

"Moving in together just makes sense and you've got the space. I think...don't walk away when I'm talking to you. I hate when you do that."

Adrian walked to his kitchen and opened the fridge. "You're not moving in."

Roberta stopped in the entryway and folded her arms. "Not yet, but soon."

He pulled out a container of cut papaya and shook his head. "I like how things are now."

"I don't."

He grabbed a fork from the drawer then sat down at the table and took the lid off the container.

"Did you hear me?"

He nodded, stabbed a cube of papaya and ate it.

"And that doesn't bother you?"

"I like you," Adrian said softly, "but I like my space more."

Roberta held up her hands in surrender. "This is not the time to talk about this. We'll talk about it later."

He took another bite. "No we won't," he said in the same soft tone.

"You're just annoyed because I keep teasing you about your music."

Adrian stabbed another cube. "You're not listening to me."

"I promise I won't do it anymore," Roberta said in a bright tone, then started to turn, but paused when she saw something on the kitchen counter. She walked over to it. "Oh, what's this?"

"Looks like a notebook," he said with little interest.

Roberta looked at the front and back of the purple notebook and shook her head. "Caryn must have left it. That woman is so detailed. You should have seen all the notes she took down when I spoke to her. I'll—"

"Leave it."

"But I should let her know—"

"I said leave it."

Roberta rested her hip on the counter and glared at him. "You really are in a mood today."

Yes, he was in a foul mood and it wasn't getting better. He hated thinking about Caryn's new love. He had to stop himself from asking what color lipstick she was wearing so he could imagine what it would be like to have her leave lipstick stains all over his chest. But she'd done the makeover for someone else, right? It wasn't for him. Although, she'd causally left part of herself in his place, was there something to that? He put the lid back on the container and sat back. "I'll take care of it."

"I thought you didn't want to have to deal with her."

He stood and put the container in the fridge.

Roberta looked at him, suddenly worried. "Is there something you don't like about her organization? If that's the case, tell me and not her. I don't—"

He closed the fridge door then said in a soft voice. "I'm not going to repeat myself." He held out his hand.

Roberta reluctantly handed him the notebook. "Fine, but promise me you won't say anything to upset her. I'd like to use her again, and—okay, okay, I know that look. I'm going." She gave him a quick kiss on the lips. "Don't mess anything up, your place looks amazing now. See you later."

Adrian waited to hear the front door close before he returned to his piano. He set the notebook down on the piano bench and stared at it. "What the hell am I doing?" He shook his head and answered himself. "You don't know, do you? I should have just given this to Roberta. Why did I decide to keep you, huh?" He tapped the notebook. "Did she leave you on purpose? No, she has someone else in her life. She probably doesn't need you anymore. Do you think you're the first? When I knew her, she had loads of you. She'd fill you up halfway and then start a new one. It used to drive me crazy," he said, his mind drifting to the past. even though he didn't want to...

"Why do you have so many notebooks?" he'd asked her, seeing a stack of them neatly sorted by color on a bookshelf in her bedroom. She lived with her aunt at the time and her room was as sparse as a nun's, which he use to tease her about.

She glanced up from her position behind her white desk. "I like to jot my ideas down with a pen. I know some people find it old fashioned but it's the only way I can organize my thoughts."

He pulled one down and flipped through it then stopped when he hit a bunch of blank pages. "You haven't finished this one yet."

"No, I haven't finished any of them."

"Why not?"

She shrugged. "I don't know. I get halfway and then want to start fresh."

He frowned, flipping through another half empty notebook. "But you're wasting paper."

"You can take some if you want."

"What would I do with half finished notebooks?"

"Use the other half? I know you could use the paper to write all your ideas in."

He was struggling financially trying to get Deadly Delectable Pies off the ground, sharing a place with Ken, not able to afford to take her out even to the movies, but she didn't complain. They went on cheap dates—bike rides, museums, free concerts and watched movies at her place, where he never left empty handed. She always packed food for him to take home—chicken patties, rice and peas, fish fritters. "I think he's only seeing you to get a free meal," he'd overheard her aunt say.

"Shh, Aunty, he might hear you."

"I hope he does. What kind of man builds a business around food and can't feed himself?"

"He's never once asked me to do this. I'm doing it because I don't want him skipping meals."

"And you love him to distraction," she said in a dry tone.

Caryn laughed. "Yes, that too."

He remembered that carefree laugh, a sound that made his heart buoyant and the note of disapproval in her aunt's voice. It was clear Barbara Lancaster didn't see much potential in him and he looked forward to the day he'd prove her wrong. "I'm not so broke that I can't buy paper," he said.

Caryn came up behind him and wrapped her arms around his waist. "You could complete them for me."

He replaced the notebook then leaned back against her, he could never be close enough. "That would be weird."

"I think it would be sweet."

He turned to her. "Sweet?"

She smiled up at him, making his body fill with a strange inner excitement. "Yes, then I'd never have to worry about wasting paper again because my brilliant boyfriend will make me proud."

He kissed her. He didn't know why, he just wanted to. No, needed to. He needed to feel the soft pressure of her lips, taste her mouth, be close to her; desperate to let her know how much he loved her. His heart, mind and soul screaming what words could not say. *Thank you for believing in me. Thank you for standing by my side. I'll make this all up to you one day.*

He couldn't remember how many notebooks he'd helped her fill up before the wedding...

Adrian let the memory fade from his mind, the sweetness of the moment making his heart heavy, and looked down at the purple notebook. "I wonder if she still..." He reached for the notebook then stopped. "I don't care." He started to play a few bars then swore. "Yes, I do care." He opened the notebook and flipped through its pages and saw she'd stopped at the halfway mark. "I knew it." He stabbed the blank page with his forefinger. "Your days are numbered. She has no use for you anymore. Welcome to the club." He snapped the notebook closed then set it down beside him. She didn't need it anymore. She wouldn't miss it.

But if she did, she'd have to come and get it.

And if she didn't, he'd give her a reason to.

CHAPTER THIRTEEN

"Cheating?" Caryn said, sending the attractive black woman a wary look.

"Yes." The woman held out her hand, the silver bracelet she wore caught the light and sparkled. "My name is Rania and you're in trouble."

"Trouble?"

"I'd prefer not to have this conversation in the hallway."

"Oh, yes. Of course." She opened the door. "Would you like anything to drink?"

"No, thank you," Rania said, making her way to the living room and taking a seat as if she were a queen about to hold court. "We're very annoyed with you right now."

"We? Is that the royal we?"

Rania gave a slight smile. "That's cute. No, I'm referring to we as in us, the other senior members of the Society."

"You're from the Black Stockings Society?"

"Yes."

Caryn sat on the love seat in front of her and clapped her hands together, pleased. "This is great! I have so many questions."

"Most of which I won't be able to answer and none that I will answer right now. You truly are in trouble."

"I don't understand. What did I do?"

Rania sent a pointed look at Caryn's trouser legs. "The stockings."

"Yes, I'm wearing them."

"Did you think you could get away with that?"

"With what?"

"No one seeing them."

"I wasn't sure they were appropriate for—"

"Do you think we would ask you to do something that would risk your professionalism?"

"No, I just—"

"Thought you could get away with bending the rules."

"There were no rules that said I had to wear the stocking with a skirt."

Rania nodded then smiled. "You're right. Maybe you don't need us after all." She stood.

"Wait, what do you mean by that?"

"We thought you were willing to live a little dangerously, but clearly..." she glanced at Caryn's legs again, "you prefer to hide."

"Does that mean I'm out?"

"No, that means you have to make up for it."

"But I haven't done anything wrong."

Rania sat and crossed her legs. "Technically, no."

"Then why am I in trouble?"

"I just told you. You're making up reasons to behave the way you've always behaved. We asked you to wear the stockings and you chose to wear them in a way so that no one could see them."

"The makeover was amazing. I feel great. I didn't think—"

"The problem is you think too much. Are you really willing to do what is necessary to get your love life out of the rut it's in?"

Caryn licked her lips, feeling like a child caught trying to feed her vegetables to the dog. 'I just didn't feel comfortable."

"I know, but that's not what I asked you. Are you willing to do what is necessary to get your love life out of the rut it's in?"

Caryn took a deep breath then said, "They just..." She hesitated, letting her words fall away.

"Weren't comfortable?"

"No, they didn't make me feel like myself."

"Or maybe they made you feel too much like yourself."

"They made me want things I shouldn't."

"The stockings don't do anything, the desire was already there. It was just reawakened."

"But—"

"You joined the club because you want your first love back."

"I didn't say that."

"Am I wrong?"

Caryn sighed. "No."

"Then you'll do as I say."

"He's already with someone else."

"Who's wrong for him," Rania said with a grin. "We both know that. And it's too late to turn back now. You can't walk away from this. You've already set things in motion and neither of you can escape unscathed."

"What things?" Caryn said startled. "I haven't—"

"So no more cheating," Rania continued.

Caryn nodded, realizing Rania wouldn't answer questions she didn't want to. "Okay."

"And you have to make up for today."

"How?"

"You'll wear the outfit I choose for you. No exceptions."

Caryn nodded. "Fine, I'll accept my punishment. When should I wear it and where?" Before Rania could reply, Caryn's mobile phone rang. "Excuse me," she said, then answered.

"Caryn," Terri said in a mild panic. "It's a big job and I need your help."

"For what?"

"You won't be alone I've already gathered a strong team. A code enforcer, the landlord, and his two sons are involved as well as a home-health nurse and a social worker."

"House or apartment?"

"House."

"And what do you need me for?"

"The kitchen."

Caryn shook her head. "You know I don't do kitchen or animal hoarders."

"We've cleaned out most of it, but the organizer I usually call is unavailable and time is running out for this man. He could lose everything. The sons really want to keep him where he is. We have to get this done tomorrow."

"Send me a video."

"I need you here. Please," she said, drawing out the word. "You know I wouldn't ask if I wasn't desperate."

Caryn squeezed her eyes shut then sighed. "Fine, I'll be there." She hung up then looked at Rania. "I'm sorry, but I have to go help a friend with a major project tomorrow."

Rania stood and grinned. "I know just what you'll wear."

"This isn't the place—" Caryn began but stopped when Rania sent her a cutting look. "Fine, what should I wear?"

THE FOLLOWING DAY, Caryn drove up to the white colonial house with black shutters and a crooked water spout, wanting to drive away for two reasons. First, she didn't want to step out of her car in the form fitting skirt and blue lace stockings Rania had her wear. Second, was the sight of one of the workers vomiting by the side of the house. She hated that the most—how people responded to the mess, at times, was worse than the mess itself. Caryn put the car in park and got out, ignoring the looks from the junk removal team.

Terri sent her a measuring look. "Aren't you a little overdressed?"

Caryn held up her hand. "Don't say anything."

"I already did. Do you have a date later or something?"

"Or something," Caryn said, feeling her face burn. She felt ridiculous.

"There's something different about you and it's not just the clothes and makeup. You seem younger and more carefree somehow. What's going on?"

More than I can say. "Nothing. I don't want to be here so let's get it over with. How many fridges?"

"Eight."

"Let me guess. Three in the kitchen, one in the living room, one in the bedroom, two in the garage and one in the backyard."

"Close," Terri said impressed. "There are two in the backyard and two in the living room. We've cleaned out most of them, the house is being aired, we actually did have a tin can of beans explode so that halted things, but the kitchen actually looks recognizable again so that's where you come in."

"Okay."

Terri handed her a mask. "You're going to need this."

Caryn didn't, but took it anyway. She was used to seeing rotting food, the smells, the sounds of maggots. It was the clutter that bothered her the most. She walked into the kitchen and saw that the countertop would need to be replaced as well as the sink. In the cupboards and pantry every shelf sagged under the weight it had to bear.

"Where's the owner?" she asked, surprised they'd

managed to get as far as they had. She was used to hearing someone outraged, shouting in distress.

"We got lucky."

Caryn clasped her hands together in delight. "He's not here?"

"Nope, a son took him and you have six hours."

No wonder they'd been able to get things done as quickly as they had. She'd worked with one client who'd spent an hour filling up a box only to spend the next hour going through it again before leaving only three items to be taken for donation.

She quickly assessed the room, listened to the information Terri provided about the owner, then worked with a carpenter to get the cabinets redone. She listed items that needed to be bought.

She didn't want to stay to see how the owner responded. Some were grateful, others angry. They would only see all that wasn't there, all the possibilities that had been taken from them. The moldy cheese that still had a good week left, the seventeenth can of tomato paste that they'd hoped to put in a casserole, the rusted pot that had been with them for years and was better than all the other pots they'd ever owned.

She'd done her best and had learned not to expect anything more. She'd tried many times to help her mother, even in later years, and had insults hurled at her instead.

"What makes you so high and mighty?" She remembered the tantrums and screaming when she'd once tossed away a stained blouse—one of two hundred—and her mother hadn't spoken to her for three days afterwards. "You need to learn to respect my things."

Caryn never told Terri the real reason why she shied away from working with animal or food hoarders. She'd never told her about Brandon, a boy she used to play with, who'd hanged himself at ten because the kids always teased him. He smelled every day. It was later that they learned why. That he lived in a house with eighty cats. They both had secrets. His worse than hers. She was never teased. She managed to keep the shower clean, she didn't care if she had to unpack it every morning to clear the new items her mother bought. Her mother was very much into appearances. Her clothes were always neatly pressed, her hair in place, and her nails were always done. It was like finding a garden of roses on the top of a pile of dung.

Brandon haunted her. She feared getting found out. She remembered hearing how his two brothers had been taken away. She didn't want to be taken, even though she wanted to be rescued.

Her mother could be so much fun at times. She was creative and she would make the best Halloween costumes. She could design hats, and shoes. She loved fashion. She was funny and smart. But they seemed to have little in common. After Caryn had cared for her uncle and never returned, her mother saw her action as a betrayal. She was cordial when they spoke now, but the accusation lay silent between them *'How could you leave me?' 'Do you think you're better than me?'*

At the end of the project the carpenter's team had

followed Caryn's design and restructured the kitchen by installing pre-fabricated cabinets and shelving.

"Thanks for this," Terri said after the final junk truck had driven away.

"No problem. Let me get away before the owner returns."

Terri glanced at the clock on her phone. "We still have time to spare. Are you going to see someone tonight?"

"No, I was just trying this outfit out."

Terri tapped something into her mobile. "You look out of place, but you look great."

"Thanks."

She paused and stared at the screen. "Umm...is there something you haven't told me?"

Aside from the fact that I was invited into a secret club? "No, I told you I got a makeover."

Terri nibbled her lower lip as she scrolled through something on the screen. "Are you sure that's all?"

"Yes."

"There wasn't a special a reason *why* you got the makeover?" she asked still fixated on the tiny screen. "You would tell me, wouldn't you?"

"Tell you what?"

Terri looked at her, worried. "Your special reason."

Caryn shook her head. "What are you talking about? Why would I need a special reason for a makeover?"

"Is it possible you did it for someone?"

"Like who?"

"Adrian."

Caryn blinked. *Was it all over her face that she couldn't stop thinking about him?* "No."

"Are you back with Adrian?"

Caryn threw her hands up, stunned. "No. Why would you think that?"

Terri turned the screen to her.

Caryn saw a video featuring Roberta then read the headline: She Organized My Life and Stole My Man.

CHAPTER FOURTEEN

Caryn watched in horror as Roberta held up a picture of her and began talking to the camera about how Caryn had ruined her life.

Caryn pointed to the screen. "She's lying. Why is she lying about me?"

"I thought you would know."

"I didn't do anything. I swear. I haven't seen him since the day I crawled out of his bathroom window."

Terri glanced at the sky. "I still can't believe you did that."

"I haven't seen him and I'm certainly not back with him."

Terri motioned to the screen. "She doesn't believe you. She thinks you and Adrian are together."

Caryn's voice cracked with outrage. "Why?"

"I don't know." Terri turned up the volume. "She's not being real specific."

"Turn it off, I don't want to hear any more."

"Aren't you curious—?"

Caryn pulled out her cell phone. "I have to talk to her." She dialed, relieved when the line picked up. "Roberta it's—"

"I know who it is," she said in a cool tone. "You have some nerve calling me."

"I'd like a chance to talk to you so we can clear up this misunderstanding."

"I didn't misunderstand a thing."

"I don't know what you think or even why, but—"

"You went behind my back and took the man I loved." Her voice rose with indignation. "The man I wanted to marry. Now I know why you changed your clothes and hair, why he wanted to give you back your notebook instead of letting me give it to you, and—"

"Notebook? Did I leave a notebook there?"

"Don't act all innocent with me."

Caryn took a deep breath. She was losing patience but getting angry wouldn't solve anything. "My new look has nothing to do with him. I really—"

"I saw it."

"What?"

"The picture."

What picture? He still had a picture of her? Doing what? Where? When? Why? "You maybe be confusing me with someone else."

"It was you."

"Then it was an old photograph. I'm sure he has pictures of other ex-girlfriends."

"No, just you."

Caryn paused. "I don't believe that."

"That's what he said."

"Then he's lying."

"No, you are." She disconnected.

Caryn gripped her hands into fists.

Terri looked at her, worried. "Let me guess...that didn't go well."

Caryn pointed to the ground. "Straight to h—"

"What are you going to do?"

Caryn grabbed her keys and marched to her car. "I'm going to see him."

CHAPTER FIFTEEN

She ended up seeing more of him than she expected to. Adrian opened the door wearing only a towel, his body still wet from a shower. "What do you want?"

Caryn watched a droplet of water slowly slide down the muscles of his chest. Another glistened on the tip of his nipple. For a moment she imagined him as a chocolate sundae she could lick. She cleared her throat. "Could you put some clothes on, please?"

He grinned. "I asked first."

She licked her lip. "You want to know why I'm here?"

He nodded.

"I have to talk to you."

He nodded again. "So talk."

"Can I at least come in?"

He motioned to the open door. "I haven't stopped you."

"I know I should have called," she said gingerly inching her way inside, making sure not to touch him; not trusting herself to touch him even accidentally. Although she'd already imagined how it would feel to have his warm, wet skin brush against hers. "But I had to see you naked," she quickly shook her head and corrected herself, "um...I mean in person."

He closed the door. "I'm listening," he said, walking in front of her.

Caryn swallowed, liking the way the rust colored towel followed with his movements, curving around his tight buns and slender hips. She briefly shut her eyes and silently swore. What was wrong with her? He was off limits. "I'll wait."

He turned to her. "For what?"

"For you to change."

A sly grin touched the corner of his mouth. "Do I make you uncomfortable?"

"It's not you. It's just." She gestured to the towel. "How can I have a serious conversation with you dressed like that?"

"I can take it off. There's nothing you haven't seen before." He reached for his towel. "Then again, maybe you've forgotten."

"No," she said, rushing forward, wrapping her arms around his waist and grabbing the towel to keep it up. Within seconds she realized her mistake, her cheek pressed against his chest, her sleeves growing moist from his wet body. She shut her eyes wanting to melt away. Her body burned from embarrassment, shame and desire.

"CeCe?" he said in a low voice.

"Yes?" she said, her voice breaking.

"I was just teasing. You can let go."

Caryn hastily stepped back, without releasing her grip, and tore off his towel. She instantly realized her mistake, staring down at the towel in horror before holding it out to him, as if holding up a curtain. Her heart raced. "I didn't see anything."

Adrian took the towel and fastened it in place. "You can open your eyes now."

She hadn't realized she'd closed them. She opened her eyes, her face and neck tingling from mortification. Why did he have this affect on her? "Right, sorry," she said, annoyed by her breathless tone.

Adrian scratched the side of his forehead and sighed sounding weary. "Just start talking. What do you want?"

"You could at least wear a robe."

He folded his arms and waited. "You're not going to win this so either talk or leave."

She sat down. "You know why I'm here. I just need you to talk to her."

"Talk to whom about what?"

"I'm not kidding, Adrian. It's not funny."

"I didn't realize I was laughing."

"I'm here because of Roberta." Caryn pulled out her mobile phone. "You need to bring her to her senses."

"I don't know what you're talking about."

She held out her phone and showed him the video.

He watched it, then swore.

"Now do you understand?" she said, putting her phone away. "How could this have happened?"

He sighed.

"Is this some sort of revenge?"

He frowned. "Revenge?"

"Yes, setting up your girlfriend to ruin my business would be one way to get back at me. You win okay? You have a right to gloat. The first time you saw me the other day, I was wearing a wig because my hair fell out. My ex-boyfriend is already with another woman. We broke up last week! My business is just gaining traction, so, this scheme—"

"You must think I have nothing better to do."

"You're right," she said, realizing how silly her accusation was. "I'm sorry. All I ask is that you talk to her."

"It won't help."

"Why not?" Caryn asked, wishing he would at least sit down so she didn't have to look up at him. "What happened?" She asked, sitting on the arm of the chair so she didn't have to look up so far. "She was so happy the last time I saw her."

He rubbed the back of his neck. "She's upset because we broke up. Relax. Things will die down soon, and the clients you want won't even pay attention to it. You always worried too much."

"I can't have her believing that you broke up because of me. You have to convince her otherwise."

"I can't. It *is* because of you."

Caryn slid off the arm of the couch and sat hard on a cushion. "What?"

"I realized I was being unfair to her and told her so. Obviously she didn't take it well and... where are you going?" he asked as she quickly left the room.

Seconds later Caryn returned with a terry robe. "You have a lot to explain."

Adrian glanced at the robe then sat down, resting his

ankle on his knee, the towel still covering him, but leaving room for her imagination to go wild. "There's not much to explain."

Caryn placed the robe on top of him like a blanket. "Why would she blame me for your break up?"

He grinned up at her. "Because it is your fault."

"But not in the way she thinks. What did you say to her?"

"I didn't have to say much when she saw the picture."

"What picture?"

"The one we took in the Caymans."

Caryn frowned. "We never went to the Caymans."

"It was fun to pretend, remember?"

Yes, she did. She remembered a tacky little hotel just outside of DC where they'd spent their first night together. The garish décor sported wallpaper with palm trees and matched the bed sheets. From the look on his face, he looked embarrassed and angry that what little money he'd scrapped together afforded them so little luxury. So she decided to make him feel better.

"Oh, it's gorgeous," she said, sweeping her hand over the bed. "I've always wanted to travel here." She walked over to the window. "Come and look at this view."

"CeCe," he said in a grim tone.

She ignored him and struggled to open the window. When she finally managed to lift it up, the sound of a roaring motorcycle filled the room. She turned to Adrian and smiled. "I just love the sound of the ocean."

His mouth twitched with amusement. "Really?"

"Yes." She held out her hand. "Come on and look at this."

"I didn't come here to look at anything but you."

Caryn looked uncertain as she walked over to the bed. "I'm not sure I can compete with the beauty of this place." She sat down on the bed and undid the top button of her blouse, sending him a coy look. "But I'll try."

He laughed in spite of himself, sitting down beside her. "You're a cruel woman," he said in a low, husky voice.

"I'll do what it takes to make you smile."

He pulled out his phone. "Let's take a picture of this," he said holding out the phone. "Where are we again?"

Caryn thought for a moment, then said, "The Caymans," and kissed him just as the camera clicked.

Caryn felt the stinging of tears as she remembered that wonderful tender night in his arms. "Why would you still have that? Shouldn't you have burned it or something?"

"I like having a memento of my biggest mistake so that I wouldn't do it again."

She quickly blinked back tears, her throat tightening at the bitterness of his words. Of course he wouldn't remember that night the way she did. To her it was still something beautiful she treasured. "I'm sorry."

Adrian folded his arms, his watchful gaze not leaving her face. "You've already said that. Many times."

Caryn gripped her hands in her lap and licked her lips. "So you won't help me?"

He briefly closed his eyes. "Don't do that."

"Do what?"

"Lick your lips like that. You always do that when you're upset or nervous."

"I do not."

"Yes, you do. Cut it out."

She held up her hands in surrender. "Fine." She pressed her hands together. "Do you want me to beg?"

"There's nothing I can do."

"Just talk to her. Please, I—"

He pointed at her. "You're doing it again."

"What?"

He motioned to her mouth. "The lips thing."

"I'm not doing it on purpose!"

He pinched the bridge of his nose. "I know," he said in a low voice. "That's what makes it worse."

"Adrian—"

"You can go to a lawyer."

"Why would I go to a lawyer when you can just go to Roberta and clear up this misunderstanding?"

He slowly stood, his gaze darkening. "How many times do I have to tell you that there was no misunderstanding?"

Caryn felt her pulse quicken. She knew that look, saw the sensual glint in his gaze, but it couldn't be. It was just her imagination. She had to focus on the situation and nothing else. She wasn't being clear, that was her problem. "Roberta thinks you cheated on her. That you left her for me."

Adrian tapped his lips and took a step towards her. "Listen to me closely. You're the reason I left her. Did you leave the notebook on purpose?"

"Wh-what?"

He took another step forward. "Did you want to have a reason to see me again?"

Caryn jumped to her feet and held out her hands. "Adrian, listen."

His gaze swept over her body. "You shouldn't have come here," he said in a low growl.

She swallowed, unsure about his feelings. He didn't look angry, he looked hungry, but that couldn't be right. "I know but—"

He stopped in front of her, so close that when he spoke his breath caressed her face. "You don't know how much I want to hate you."

"I understand—"

He shook his head. "No, I don't think you do." He cupped her chin. "You must think I'm crazy. Because I'd have to be crazy to fall for you again." He brushed the back of his fingers, in a feather light caress, against her cheek. "I'd have to be insane to let you get close to me." His hand slid to her neck. "Delusional and completely out of my mind to even think you're good for me." He covered her mouth with his, sending her senses spinning. "But I'm not insane," he whispered against her lips.

"No," she breathed, startled that she'd been right about him. That she hadn't misread his look.

"And I won't let you get close," he said, holding her tighter.

"I know."

"Unless..."

She froze. Had it been a trick? Was he toying with her emotions? "Unless what?" she said with caution, preparing herself for an insult.

"Unless you say you did it for me." He kissed her neck, letting his hands slide down her waist to her thighs. "Say you did it all for me."

Did what? What did he mean? "Yes," she lied.

He grinned. "I knew it. When Roberta told me about your makeover and then you left your notebook I guessed it was a sign."

"Yes," Caryn said, not knowing what else to say.

"But I still wasn't sure until you arrived looking like this." His gaze slid slowly down her body, his heated gaze lingering on her stocking clad legs with masculine pleasure. "That's when I knew."

Caryn's heart fluttered like a trapped bird. "I wasn't sure you'd like it." She licked her bottom lip. "I know I've changed."

He held her gaze his voice deepening with feeling. "You're still beautiful to me."

It was a dream. In a minute she'd wake up and be alone in her room. Adrian couldn't really be looking at her like that and saying what she'd hoped to hear.

"CeCe?"

He sounded real. He felt real. This was real. But she didn't know what to say. It all felt so wonderful she didn't want to do anything to spoil it.

"I like your stockings. Do you have panties to match?"

She felt some of her paralysis fading. He was teasing her; she could tease him back. "Maybe. Do you want to see?"

He shook his head.

She blinked surprised. "Really?"

"Yes, I don't want to see them. I want to take them off."

She unbuttoned her blouse. "Be patient."

Adrian swept her up in his arms. "No," he said then placed her on the couch.

Caryn pointed down the hall. "I thought your bedroom was that way."

"I don't think I can make it," he said, unbuttoning her blouse then pushing it away. His hand slid between her breasts and down her stomach. "I've waited so long for this." He unlatched her bra and gazed at her chest. "Why did she keep me away from you for so long?" he said like a man deprived, before covering one breast with his mouth and then the other. "I'll never let her keep us apart again."

"Do you expect them to reply?" Caryn said amused by his interest.

"Oh they're replying," he said, teasing one hard nipple with his tongue. "We understand each other perfectly. Intimately," he said, teasing the other. He unzipped her skirt then slid it down her legs. "But I don't want her to be jealous." He slid off her stockings. "Don't worry baby, you have my full attention." He cupped her center. "Have you missed me? Yes, I know you have."

Caryn felt her body grow more aroused but didn't want him to have all the fun. She let her hand sneak under his towel. "I've missed him too," she said taking hold.

"He's glad to hear it."

"But he's a little under dressed for this party."

"Under dressed?"

"This party requires a coat. Of course he doesn't have to enter. I can entertain him in other ways."

"Let go and don't move."

"I'm finding it hard..." she tenderly squeezed and toyed with the tip of him, "...to let go of you."

Adrian took a deep shuddering breath. "Try. I want to come inside you. You owe me that."

Caryn slid her hand up and down. "But this feels so good."

He closed his eyes and gritted his teeth. "CeCe, I'm serious."

"Me too," she said then led him inside her.

He swore. "Wait, I'm not—"

"I'm making an exception," she said, tightening herself around him. "You feel even better now."

He eased further inside her, his hard body atop hers. "You're playing a dangerous game."

But it wasn't a game. She wanted him back and she wanted him to know it. Shivers of delight followed his every caress. Ecstasy followed the taste and touch of his lips. Desire and passion erased the years that had kept them apart until she felt that nothing had changed, everything was familiar, everything was right. This was their chance to be together forever. "Marry me," she whispered.

He paused.

She froze, feeling the tension in him. Silence suddenly filling the room like a heavy mist, crackling with anticipation. She couldn't take the words back, perhaps he hadn't heard her. She squeezed her eyes shut, berating herself. She'd acted out of character. She wasn't being sensible. She was asking for too much too soon. She'd gotten greedy and he had a right to be angry. "I'm—"

He pressed a finger over her lips. "Don't say you're sorry. Did you mean it?"

She swallowed, for the first time unable to read his expression, for the first time seeing how much of a man he'd become in eight years. He wasn't just older, but more in control of his emotions, more guarded. His dark, intense gaze gave nothing away, offering no hint to what he wanted her to say. Did he think she was mocking him? Would he laugh and say marrying her was the last thing he'd do? Or did he want her to say yes? Did he want to hear that she loved him still? She took a deep breath then said, "Yes."

He shook his head.

She shriveled up inside, ashamed that she'd asked him at such an intimate moment. There was nowhere to hide. "Of course you won't," she said with a slight laugh. "I shouldn't have—"

"I didn't say that."

"But you shook your head."

"Because you asked the wrong question." He nuzzled her neck and she could hear the smile in his voice. "You know I'll marry you." Her captured her eyes again. "But will *you* marry *me*?"

It was a fair question and her first response was to say yes, but she could understand his hesitation. She'd said yes to him before. She wanted to ask him if he'd truly forgiven her, could reconciliation be this easy? Did he really love her still? But she knew now wasn't the time for more questions, only answers. "Yes," she said.

He released a long sigh, as if he'd been holding his breath.

She stared at him, surprised. "You didn't think I'd say yes?"

"It took you long enough to say anything."

She drew him closer. "Maybe because I'm tired of speaking." She kissed him and with her kiss she silently said, I never thought you'd forgive me.

And his low moan said, It wasn't easy.

Her hands roamed intimately over his body saying, I'll make it up to you.

And as he stoked the passionate fire within her, causing her body to vibrate with liquid ecstasy he made his claim silently saying, You'll have a lifetime to try because I won't let you go.

Soon nothing more needed to be said silent or otherwise, their entwined bodies moving rhythmically to the love beating within their hearts. A love that had only grown stronger and threatened to overtake her completely.

CHAPTER SIXTEEN

Caryn stared at her reflection in the mirror. Only a week ago she'd been standing in Adrian's bathroom ready to escape and now...now she was going to marry him. She stared at her reflection not sure of the woman she saw. She didn't look like the woman from a week ago, or the woman who'd walked out of Haven Spa. This woman looked radiant, vibrate in love. Yes, that's what it was. Love. It was thrilling and made her feel alive. She was in love and a little frightened, but she'd hold on tight. Hold on to him and the promises they shared.

She reapplied her lipstick, left the bathroom, and found Adrian at the piano. He'd changed into a pair of jeans and a striped black and orange T-shirt. He ran his fingers above the keys without touching them.

"Your place or mine?" he said.

Caryn stared at him stunned. "We just did it at your place."

The corner of his mouth kicked up in amusement. "I meant, will we live at your place or mine?"

She sat down beside him and playfully nudged him with her elbow. "You could have phrased that differently."

He playfully nudged her in return. "I know. Do you want to get a house?"

"No, I think your place is good for now." She watched his silent performance then said, "I love this song."

His face split into a wide grin. "I thought you would."

"Still playing those honky tonk songs?"

His smile slowly faded. He nodded.

"Then why aren't you playing one now?"

"I know you hate them."

"I never said that." She tugged on his goatee. " I teased you because it was fun, but I was glad they made you happy. Especially since you were working so hard back then, I was afraid you'd burn yourself out."

He began to play then said in a low Kentucky drawl. "I done good?"

"Yes, boy. You done made yo mama proud."

He winced.

"What?"

"You still can't do a Southern accent."

"Don't be mean. That was good."

"Yes, if you wanted to sound like a West Indian who got lost in the Bronx."

"Says the man whose father was a professional cricket player."

Adrian tapped the side of his head. "I have an ear for various American accents."

"And I don't?"

He winked at her. "Don't worry, love, I'll marry you anyway."

Caryn's cell phone rang, interrupting her reply. "Saved by the bell."

"You don't have to answer. You can continue to argue with me and lose."

She walked over to her handbag and picked up her phone. "I know," she said, recognizing the ring tone for her brother, Roland. She sighed. "But I have to take this."

"Go ahead."

"It won't take long."

Adrian sent her an odd look. "You don't have to explain." He nodded to the phone in her hand. "Go on."

But she felt she did have to explain. If only he knew what her brother's phone calls usually meant. Maybe she'd be wrong this time. She answered. "What is it?"

"Mom's acting strange."

Nope, she was right. "And that's news because...?"

"Someone needs to talk to her."

Caryn sat down and lowered her voice. "And you think that someone should be me?"

"Either you talk to Mom or you talk to Ella."

She stiffened. "Why would I need to talk to her?"

"Her husband just called me. He's threatening divorce."

Caryn silently swore. Roland always referred to Louis as 'her husband,' never believing that the union between the two would last long. "I'll talk to her, you talk to Mom."

"I think—"

"Let me just talk to her first before we make any decisions. Is she at work?"

"Yes."

"Okay, I'll call you later." She hung up. "I'm afraid I have to go."

He stood up from the piano and walked over to her. "Is something wrong?"

Very. "I have to call my sister," she said, grabbing her handbag. "Just regular family stuff." She made sure to keep her voice light although her heart felt heavy.

He rested his hands on his hips. "Just answer me one thing."

"What?"

"Do you have any regrets?"

I wish I didn't have to go. I wish I could spend all day and night with you. "About us?"

He nodded.

There was a lethal calmness in his eyes, as if he were asking her another, deeper question. "No," she said, kissing him lightly on the lips. "I got exactly what I came for," she lied, wanting him to believe that she'd come for the notebook and seduced him with her clothes, then realized she hadn't gotten what she'd wanted and silently swore. They still hadn't resolved the Roberta issue. Now that they were a couple, Roberta would believe he'd cheated.

"I'll handle the video," Adrian said as if reading her thoughts.

"Thank you."

"Come back for dinner."

She headed for the door. "I'll see if I can."

"What's going on?"

Her footsteps slowed. "Nothing, I just told you—"

"Don't lie to me."

She turned to him. She didn't want to lose him, but couldn't tell him the truth yet. "It's something to do with my sister. I'll explain it...later. Not now. Please don't force me to talk about it now."

"All right. Come back tonight. I don't care how late."

Caryn hesitated.

"I'm not hearing a yes."

"I can't make any promises."

He fell silent then said, "Is this the reason why you left me the first time?"

Caryn opened the door. "I told you, I'll explain later."

He nodded. "Fine, but I'm not as patient as I used to be."

CHAPTER SEVENTEEN

Every time Caryn stepped into her sister's airy, beautifully decorated consignment shop, she felt like running out again. Stores like this were one of their mother's greatest weaknesses. Although no bell chimed when she stepped in, her sister immediately turned, alert to any possibility of a sale. When she saw it was her sister, her bright smile of greeting dimmed.

"Either smile or meet me outside," she said in a low voice. "I can't have customers thinking you're going to be ill."

Caryn nodded and left the store and waited. She glanced out at the crowded parking lot of the busy shopping center, watched a woman carrying two large fake plants from the craft store on one side and smelled the scent of baked bread and chocolate chip cookies that wafted through the door of the sandwich shop next door.

"What is it?" Ella said, coming outside.

"Roland called me."

Her eyes widened with fear. "What's happened to Mom?"

"He called me about you."

She folded her arms. "What about me?"

"Louis is threatening divorce this time. What did you do?"

"Where's the extra money coming from?"

"What?"

She gestured to Caryn's clothes. "Do you really need me to price what you're wearing right now? I'll start with the shoes."

Caryn rubbed her nose. "I've been saving."

Ella narrowed her eyes. "You save, but you don't splurge, especially on things. What are you hiding?"

Caryn tilted her head to the side. "Do you think changing the subject is going to save your marriage?"

Ella squinted at a red jeep pulling out of a parking space. "It's no big deal."

"What did you do?"

She sighed then turned to her. "Louis found out that I have a storage unit he didn't know about."

Caryn leaned her head back in despair. "Ella, you already have two."

"I needed more space," she said without apology. "You wouldn't believe the amount of merchandise I receive and—"

"You're still shopping, aren't you?"

"It's my money and it's not as bad as it once was."

"How big is the unit?"

"It's not that big."

"Give me a number."

"It's not that much."

Caryn slowed her words. "How big?"

"Ten by fifteen."

Caryn leaned back. "You're out of control, Ella."

Ella pulled her forward. "I just had the window cleaned," she said checking for possible smudges."

"Ella."

"And don't you just love my new display?" She smiled up at the two well dressed mannequins—one in a spring dress, the other in an evening gown.

"Ella, you have to address this."

"I'm in perfect control."

"Mom—"

Ella spun to her, anger in her eyes. "Don't you dare. I'm not one of your clients. Louis is just upset because I kept a secret from him. That's all. I'll apologize."

"He's getting fed up with—"

"He loves me too much. He won't leave me."

"Ella, you know I'm here for you."

A sour smile touched her lips. "There's that tone again. That condescending, patronizing tone. That tone that says 'I'm better than everyone else so let me fix you.'"

"That's not true."

"Do you think living in your minimalist townhouse, with no clutter, no object out of place means that your life isn't a mess? For years I wondered why you let Adrian go, a man so wonderful even I was half in love with him, but now I know. It's because you're afraid to hold on to anything." Ella turned and gripped the door handle to her store. "My life is full and rich and maybe a little messy," she said opening the door. "But it's mine."

***

MINIMALIST.

Caryn sat in her living room staring at her space with new eyes. She had her living room set, but no bookshelves, just those in her office where she kept her notebooks, but she didn't own books. She borrowed them from the library, no collectibles, few pictures, two paintings spaced evenly apart. She didn't need to own things like books, music or movies. She rarely entertained, so she didn't need a wine cellar like her friend...or vases for flowers or plants. A simple life. That's the world she'd created for herself. Not because she was scared. And, although she'd let Adrian go, she'd gotten him back again.

Adrian. She'd told him she'd explain, but she couldn't share too much, not yet. She sent him a text that she'd see him tomorrow, hoping he wouldn't be too disappointed, although sending the text broke her heart.

CHAPTER EIGHTEEN

"My sister is a shopaholic," Caryn told Adrian the following evening, as the flames of a dozen candles glowed against the darkness. She hadn't expected the romantic mood when he'd invited her for dinner—the living room picnic of fresh rolls, shrimp scampi, and wine; the petals of red roses scattered along the white blanket—but as she entered his apartment, she'd felt a sense of resolve. She could balance her two worlds and keep them separate. She'd practiced her explanation on her drive to his place, hoping that when she said it, she didn't give away how severe her sister's compulsion was. She looked at him, the candlelight highlighting the sharp angles of his jaw and continued in a nonchalant tone, "And her husband's threatening divorce. I was trying to help her."

He lowered his gaze and rubbed his thumb against the stem of his wine glass. "Are you sure it isn't something else?"

"What do you mean?"

He lifted his gaze. "I want us to be honest with each other."

My mother is a hoarder and my sister...has tendencies. The real reason I had to meet with her is because she's bought another large storage unit without telling her husband. Right now my brother is dealing with my mother because she's not acting like herself and that's saying a lot. And my sister thinks I'm afraid to hold onto things so I may have issues as well. Do you still want to marry me? "I am being honest."

"Do you know why I did this?" he asked gesturing to the scene.

"Because you're a romantic?"

"No, because I wanted you to remember the first time I did it."

Caryn couldn't help a smile as the memory filled her thoughts. "Yes, but it wasn't this grand. You'd managed to kick Ken out of your cramped apartment for a couple of hours and you'd bought...what were they? They're like the cheapest flower."

"They weren't that cheap."

She pointed at him. "Carnations!" she said with a laugh. "But they'd been dyed red or something and I remember the candles." She tapped her chin, thoughtful. "And you'd made this large pizza and had the red peppers arranged in the shape of a heart."

"You remember that very well," he said pleased.

"I remember every moment."

"Do you remember what you wrote in your note to me?"

Her voice faltered. "Of course."

"What did you say?"

He'd caught her. She licked her lip. "I don't remember it word for word."

"It was important," he said, his tone soft, seeming to mirror the darkness. "Don't you think you'd remember the gist of it?"

"It was so painful I blocked it out."

"Or maybe you don't remember because it was a lie."

"Do we have to talk about that now?" she said forcing a smile. She let her finger trail over the surface of one of the petals. "I thought we wanted to move forward." She scooped up some petals then let them fall from her fingers. "Forget the past."

His expression didn't change. "That phone call yesterday changed things. I watched you, CeCe. You couldn't leave my place fast enough."

"I admit that I'm worried about my sister."

His tone deepened. "You're worried about something else too."

Not now. I can't talk about it now. "Let's not ruin this moment."

"I need to resolve this. If it made you run from me once, it may again." He lifted a brow. "You still don't remember what you wrote?"

Caryn searched her mind, frantically trying to remember the excuse she'd used for leaving him all those years ago. She remembered wanting to make him angry. Wanting him to hate her. Or at least give him a reason to stay away. What had she said? Slowly images began to come together. She saw Ken being nervous about an investment deal falling through, Adrian's sister telling him that he couldn't afford to get married. Money. His problem was always money. She'd used it somehow.

Debt. Yes. She'd told him that she was drowning in debt and that she'd hid it from him and didn't want him to be tied to her because of it. She wrote how ashamed she was for deceiving him. That she couldn't wait for him to make it, that she liked to spend money now. She'd written that he was better off without her.

"You remember now?" he asked, studying her.

"Yes."

"Will the debt return?"

Caryn hung her head. His question made it clear that he knew her excuse was a lie. He made it sound as if it was someone rather than something. "No."

"How can I be sure?"

She reached out and took his hand. "Because I'm older now and I'm tired of running. I won't let anything come between us."

Adrian reached into his pocket and pulled out a ring then slid it on her finger. "That's a promise I plan to hold you to."

Caryn stared down at the round-cut, white gold, diamond ring, amazed by how glorious his ring felt on her finger. "You bought me an engagement ring already?"

"Why wait?"

She lifted her gaze to his face. "I thought you'd want to keep us a secret for a while."

His compelling brown eyes held her still. "You thought wrong."

CHAPTER NINETEEN

They had hoped never to meet again.

Barbara Lancaster watched as Hazel Everett, wearing a blue dress that had suffered one wash too many, made her way to the table located by the window of the tearoom. One of the few in the county, let alone the state, but Barbara despised the smell of coffee and abhorred the thought of meeting in a cafe. However, the charming setting of white table cloths and silver trays filled with tea cakes didn't help her mood. She wished to be elsewhere, but her smile of greeting gave nothing away.

"I'm glad you could make it," she said as her companion approached the table.

"I didn't have a choice," Hazel said, taking a seat.

"So, I assume he's told you."

"About him and...and...her," Hazel said stumbling over the last word, making it clear she had a hard time addressing Caryn by name, even less as a pronoun. "Yes, he did."

Barbara's mood improved a fraction, pleased that Adrian's mother was just as upset as she was about the situation. "I didn't expect it to come to this."

"We have to do something to stop them."

"Which is why I called you," Barbara said, pouring her some tea. "To make sure we're both in agreement."

"Of course." Hazel added sugar to her tea. "I haven't changed how I feel." She nosily stirred it, letting her spoon hit the side of the cup, as if she were playing the triangle and calling a large work crew in for dinner. "They can't be together, it—"

"Don't upset yourself," Barbara said, resisting the urge to snatch the spoon away. To think this woman had bred children, she thought tasting the tart crumbs of bitterness. She'd never had the opportunity, although she and her husband had tried for years. She would have made a perfect mother, unlike her sister. Her sister had wasted her chance, but providence had given her Caryn.

Caryn was the daughter she should have had. She'd come into her life just when she needed her, becoming the daughter she'd always wanted to have. Caryn was her chance to be the mother she was meant to be. And as a mother she had to protect her from a family that also had a stain of mental illness in their bloodline. Adrian was unsuitable because of his hold on her. She didn't like his power over Caryn and she'd fight to keep him away.

"How can I not be upset? I find the entire thing upsetting. What is wrong with him? How could he even think of going back to her? Has he no pride?"

"Your tea is getting cold."

"What?"

Barbara nodded to Hazel's teacup, which had managed to survive her continual banging. "I think it's been properly stirred."

"Oh yes," she said then set the spoon down and slurped her tea.

Barbara reached for a teacake wondering which sound she hated more. "I'm afraid my niece can be very convincing and she's undergone a makeover. That may have persuaded him to change his mind."

"We need to change it back. She's after his money."

Barbara's tone cooled. "My niece is not mercenary."

"I'm sorry," Hazel said quickly, realizing her error. "It's just so frustrating."

"Yes, we both want the same thing. I was able to stop her last time—"

"And you think you can do it again?" Hazel rushed to finish, her brown eyes bright with hope.

"No, I think you may need to do it this time."

Hazel's hope dimmed. "What can I do?"

A sly smile touched Barbara's lips. "I have a few ideas."

CHAPTER TWENTY

"I can't let you do this," Terri said, watching Caryn model a form fitting red dress in front of her bedroom mirror.

"I'll wear another color."

Terri pounded her fist on the bed. "I'm not talking about the dress. You can't get back with Adrian."

"I already am. And he's invited me to be his date for an important event. I can't let him down."

"You're making a mistake."

"You're the one who said I wasn't over him and you were right."

"I was trying to encourage you to find someone else," Terri said her voice nearly a whine. "Not go running back to him."

"I didn't run."

"Please don't do this." She held up Caryn's hand and pointed to the ring. "This is probably a trick."

"The diamond is real."

Terri shoved her hand away and scowled. "You're pretending not to understand me on purpose."

"We're getting married. Nothing has changed. I love him as much now as I did then."

"You're giving him a chance to break your heart. What if this is all an act? The words, the dinner, the sex." She held up a finger when Caryn opened her mouth. "And don't tell me how real it was because I don't want to know."

"He's not acting."

"You don't know that. You just want it to be true." She leaned forward, her voice urgent. "What if he plans to dump you on your wedding day the way you did him?"

"He won't. He's forgiven me."

"You don't know that. It's been eight years Caryn. Eight years. You don't know what he's like now."

"He's the same."

"Sleeping with him isn't the same as knowing him."

"We're planning our life together. I agreed to sign a prenup—"

"See?" Terri said, making a smug gesture. "He doesn't want you to have access to his money."

"I offered because I want to show him that I'm not after his money," she clarified, returning to her reflection.

"You're being naïve. You need to test him to make sure his heart is really yours. It's all happening too fast just like it happened all those years ago. You're following your heart instead of your head." She glanced down. "What is that?"

"What?"

Terri bent down and looked under the bed. "My foot

just hit something. You don't usually keep things under your bed." She pulled out a box.

"It's nothing." Caryn said, wishing she'd hidden her box somewhere else. What if Terri opened it and asked her questions? What should she say? What did other members do when someone found out? She snatched the box from her. "Don't look."

Terri looked at her startled. "Why not?"

"It's a birthday gift."

"My birthday already passed."

"For next year," Caryn corrected, tucking it on a high shelf in her closet.

Terri shook her head. "Sometimes I'm not sure I know you anymore. The closet full of clothes, returning to your ex. And those stockings look dangerous."

Caryn felt the same way. Her third pair were the most daring of her selection—a triangle patterned dark black pair with bold silver thread. She didn't know how to explain them away, but didn't want to.

"What's gotten into you?" Terri continued then shook her head. "No, don't answer that. Answer this. Is Adrian really the one making you this happy? Making you glow with a beauty I haven't seen for years?"

Caryn turned to her friend, bit her lip and nodded.

Terri sighed. "Then I just wished I wasn't so afraid for you."

Caryn rested her hands on her shoulders, seeing the concern in her eyes. "Me too. I'm scared of being this happy, to be this much in love again. But I won't fight it. I can't. Yes, something has come over me. I've got a second chance and I'm not letting go."

ADRIAN DEBATED whether he should laugh or take a picture as he stared at his sister, Monica, who stood in front of his door with her arms out wide, blocking him from leaving his apartment. Strands of hair escaped from her ponytail and she stood on her tiptoes, although that didn't make much difference since he was over a foot taller than she was. "I'm not going to let you do this."

Adrian pulled on his jacket, realizing it was his mistake to let her drop by in the first place, but she'd told him she'd found a place for the bears. "You're going to make me late."

"I don't care. I admit that I didn't like Roberta, but I'd prefer you with her than crawling back to Caryn."

Adrian folded his arms. "She came to me."

"When Mom told me you were planning to marry her, she broke down and cried."

"Mom only cries when she wants something from Dad." Adrian pushed his sister aside and opened the door.

Monica slammed it closed, fell to the ground then stretched the width of it. "I can't watch you go back to her."

"Then close your eyes." He gripped the door handle.

She pushed to keep the door closed. "You're my little brother and I'm trying to protect you. You shouldn't be with her at all. That woman should come with a warning label. She humiliated you and broke your heart."

He managed to open the door, pushing her away with it. "I'm going."

She grabbed his leg instead. "No. Don't do this."

He shook his leg. "Let go."

"Not until you come to your senses."

He glared down at her. "I don't want to hurt you."

"Then listen to me."

Adrian started walking down the hall, dragging her with him.

"How do you know she really loves you?" Monica continued, keeping her hold. "How do you know she won't run away from you again?"

He kept walking.

"Ow! You're giving my thigh rub burn."

He glanced down at her denim skirt, unfazed. "Then let go."

"Are you thinking of revenge? A little payback? That's it, right? You're going to give her a taste of her own medicine."

He pinched the back of her neck, forcing her to let go. She yelped out in pain then grabbed his coat sleeve, ripping it. He stared at the torn sleeve then stared at her. "Are you crazy?"

"You should ask her," Monica shot back. "She knows about it more than I do."

His gaze sharpened. "What do you mean?"

Monica hung her head suddenly embarrassed. "Nothing."

He seized her elbow and dragged her back to his apartment. "Start talking," he said, taking off his jacket and heading to his bedroom.

"It's n—"

Adrian crumpled the jacket into a ball. "Say 'nothing' again and I'm going to stuff this thing in your mouth."

Monica sat on the bed. "It's just that...crazy seems to run in her family."

He opened his closet and grabbed another jacket. "Crazy seems to run in a lot of families," he said, giving her a significant look.

"I'm talking real crazy. Mental illness kind of crazy."

"How do you know that?"

"I don't...all right, all right," she said when he picked up the torn coat and began to ball it up. "I found out through Mom. She didn't want you to know."

"Know what?"

"About Caryn's family. She spoke to Caryn's Aunt Barbara. Mom wouldn't go into details, but mentioned that Caryn's decision was best for both of you and we agreed."

"What do you mean 'we' agreed?"

Monica bounced

to her feet. "Gosh, look at the time."

Adrian pushed her back down. "Who is 'we'?"

"I thought you didn't want to be late."

He lowered his voice, his expression darkening. "I'm not going to ask you again."

"I didn't know until after it happened, but Mom and Caryn's aunt convinced Caryn that marrying you wasn't the right thing."

"Are you telling me Mom knew that Caryn would leave me?"

"She'd begged her to call it off. She didn't think she

would go that far, that's what upset her the most. She was supposed to cancel before that day, but she fooled us."

"Fooled you?"

"Yes, she took it too far. That's why you can't trust her. You don't know what she'll do."

Monica kept talking, but Adrian didn't hear the rest of her words. Instead he remembered the look on Caryn's face that day. The expression in her eyes. He hadn't understood it before, couldn't interpret it, but now he could. "I'm sorry. I can't," she'd said, and now he saw the pain, the regret, the guilt that came with her words. It seemed to have come out of nowhere, but now it all made sense. He'd remembered her looking briefly into the crowd and how her expression changed. What had his mother said to her? What was she hiding?

"It's getting late," Monica said. "You'd better call her and cancel."

"I'm not canceling anything," Adrian said, leaving his bedroom. "And you'd better call Mom to warn her." He opened the front door.

Monica followed him into the hall. "Warn her?"

He turned and sent her a dark look. "Yes, that she's going to hear from me."

CHAPTER TWENTY-ONE

"If you're not feeling well, we could have cancelled," Caryn said in a low tone, casting a nervous look at Adrian's tight jaw and grim expression as they stood in the ballroom of the annual spring gala. He'd apologized to her for running late, saying he'd eaten something that hadn't agreed with him, but she felt there was more to it than that.

She hadn't had a chance to talk to him alone since they'd entered the event. It was the first time she got to see the extent of his success. It went way beyond his expensive apartment or even the ring on her finger. He was a man of status and power and people flocked to him with evident admiration. She didn't mind being in his shadow, pleased to see how far he'd come. He carried himself with an easy confidence she knew had been hard won, but despite his smiles and laughter, she sense something was wrong.

It was when they had a rare moment alone that she asked him the question and he was slow to answer. Casting a wave and a smile at a couple before he answered. "I want to be with you tonight," he said, nodding at another guest.

"Could have fooled me."

He turned to her, startled. "Really?"

She laughed at his expression. "You don't look happy, not that anyone else would really notice, but I know you too well."

"It's not you," he said, his gaze suddenly intense. "I'm glad you're here. You're so beautiful." His gaze softened into tenderness. He brushed his lips against hers, leaving her wanting more. "I just wish...I wish we'd gotten back together sooner."

"And you blame me for that."

He shook his head. "No, now that I know...I mean. No, it's not that." He glanced up as if searching for a reason to look away. "I see Ken."

Caryn stiffened. She knew she'd meet people from the past but she wasn't sure she was ready.

"It's going to be okay," Adrian said as they walked over to him.

Caryn felt her heartbeat quicken with every step. Ken had his back to them, but still had the tall arrogant stance she remembered, his black hair slicked down.

"Hey, Ken," Adrian said, resting a hand on his shoulder. "I wasn't sure you'd come."

Ken spun around with a smile, which slowly faded when he spotted Caryn. "I see you came alone. Where's Roberta?"

Adrian's expression changed. "Don't make me embarrass you."

"I don't embarrass easily." He flashed a cruel smile. "I guess we have that in common." He shoved his hands in his pockets. "But I can tell by that look that you don't think I'm being polite. Okay." He leaned towards Caryn and said in a soft voice. "Will you please give my friend back his balls?"

Adrian lunged at him. "You son of a—"

Caryn jumped between them and said in a low voice. "Not here. Please. People are starting to stare."

The two men held each other's gaze.

"We're used to stares, aren't we?" Ken said. "When you left him, I was right by his side as everyone stared at him standing at the altar."

Adrian grabbed his arm. "Don't disrespect—"

"Adrian it's okay," Caryn said quickly. "He has a right to feel the way he does."

Ken shot her a glance. "Thanks for the permission."

"I didn't mean..."

"But I don't blame you." Ken lightly tapped the side of Adrian's face. "He's better looking now that he's got money."

Adrian grabbed Ken's hand. "You're itching for me to break your fingers."

Caryn seized his arm. "Let's go."

Ken sent her a significant look. "Yes, please do."

Adrian didn't move.

Caryn tugged at Adrian's sleeve. "I want to go."

Adrian shoved his friend away and let her lead him to the hall.

"I shouldn't have come."

"He has no right talking to you like that."

"Yes, he does. He's your friend and he loves you. He knows how much I hurt you."

"He didn't just disrespect you. He disrespected me."

"No, he—"

"You're my woman. My choice. And he's trying to tell me who I should be with." He glanced up at the sky as if he could find the answers in the stars. "First my mom and now him."

Caryn frowned. "What about your mom?"

Adrian shook his head. "Never mind." He swore. "I need a drink."

"That's a good idea. You go get a drink."

"And where will you go?" Adrian asked when Caryn headed in another direction.

"I want to talk to Ken."

"Okay, we'll both get a drink first."

She shook her head. "No, I want to talk to him alone."

"Ken's got a temper."

"I know."

"If he makes you cry..."

"He won't." She kissed him in reassurance. "Trust me."

CARYN DIDN'T HAVE a problem finding Ken again. He was enjoying the company of five ladies who appeared to find everything he said fascinating. She tapped him on the shoulder. "Could I talk to you for a moment?"

"Excuse me, ladies," he said, then slowly turned and walked past her. "I'm going out for a smoke, you can follow if you want." Once outside in the portico of the hotel, he took out a pack and lit a cigarette. A warm spring darkness seeped past the lighting of the building, casting shadows along the brick path and bushes.

"I hurt everyone back then, and I am truly sorry," Caryn said, knowing her words sounded hollow, but having nothing else to say.

"Really?" Ken narrowed his eyes through the haze of smoke. "It took you eight years to figure that out?"

"I know how you feel."

He took a long drag then exhaled. "No, you don't. We all loved you. We thought you were the best thing to happen to Adrian. Especially me." He tapped his chest. "I still remember the day he told me he'd met the woman he was going to marry. I think he'd only known you a month by then. I'd never seen him so happy. Then you left him...on his wedding day." He took another long drag of his cigarette and exhaled, the smoke spiraling up before it disappeared. "Let me paint you a picture. There's this man standing in front of his family and friends ready to make one of the biggest steps in his life. No one else knew this, but he didn't even sleep the night before. That's how excited he was."

"Ken, you don't have to tell me—"

"And then when he saw the love of his life coming towards him he couldn't stop smiling and I teased him and said 'Are you ready for this?' and he just said 'Lock and load', which meant he was ready for anything. But I knew I didn't need to ask the question, because he'd told me he'd been waiting for that moment his whole life." He took another long drag. "Yeah, the damn bastard can be stupid like that."

"Ken, really I—"

He waved his cigarette. "I haven't gotten to the best part yet. The part when she looked up at him, holding his hand in hers and whispered, 'I can't do this,' then ran down the aisle without looking back. She packed her things and disappeared. Didn't answer any of his calls or texts. She sent him a letter. I don't know if he read it or not, just told me he got one and that was it." Ken stubbed out his cigarette on the side of a trash bin then dropped it inside.

"I've only seen my buddy cry twice," he continued. "First, when a cousin of his drowned and then because of you. He was stunned at first. He didn't cry when it happened. We just got drunk that night and talked about what a *puta* you were. How much better off he was without you. And for a time he seemed fine then, it was a year later, on what would have been your first year anniversary, we were riding in the park and saw a wedding party.

"Adrian rode past it and then stopped when he saw a white deflated balloon on the ground with the words 'just married' printed on it. He picked it up and this older woman sees us, smiles and says 'Congratulations' and I started to laugh, but he just lost it." Ken folded his arms. "I'm not going to tell you what happened because it's none of your damn business, but I'll say this. The second time we got drunk over you it wasn't just the liquor that flowed."

Caryn sighed feeling the weight of Ken's disgust. "I hurt him. I realize that."

"But if you knew how much you wouldn't be standing in front of me right now, batting those pretty brown eyes of yours and asking forgiveness."

"I know it won't be easy, but I'll work at earning your trust again."

"Why does it matter?"

"Because you matter to him and your opinion is important."

"You mean, you know I have an influence." A reluctant smile touched his lips. "Yes, you always were smart."

"Ken—"

"But it takes more than smarts to fix this. No, you just left him. And now you're back and we're all supposed to forget how you treated him because you love him so much? He may be blinded by his love for you, but I'm not because you left him when he needed you most. Where were you when we were building our business? When he wasn't sure he could make payroll? When the cash didn't come? When he failed?"

"I can't make up for the past," Caryn said in a helpless tone.

Ken shook his head. "No, that's what scares me the most. You can. I looked at my friend and he has that same look in his eye that he had all those years ago. You're the only one who's ever been able to put that kind of joy on his face and that's what worries me."

"I won't hurt him again."

"You can't promise me that."

"I need him as much as he needs me."

"No, he needs you more." Ken turned to the door where a looming silhouette stood. "He doesn't want to lose you and that gives you the upper hand."

"I love him."

"I don't believe you." Ken rested a hand on her shoulder, leaned in and whispered, "But I'll give you a chance to prove me wrong," he said before he walked away.

Adrian approached her. "What did he say to you?"

Caryn wrapped her arms around his waist, glad the ordeal was over. "That I'd better treat you right."

He searched her face unconvinced. "That doesn't sound like him."

"I read between the lines."

Adrian wrapped his arms around her. "And what did you say to him?"

"That I'll try really hard."

He kissed her forehead. "You always make me hard."

Caryn covered his mouth with her hand, outraged. "Don't say things like that."

He removed her hand. "No one can hear me. And if they did, they'd be jealous. I'm a happy man right now. No, don't move."

"Why not?"

"Because I'm still *really* happy right now."

Caryn glanced down at the front of his trousers. "You're joking."

"No, I'm not. You can't see out here, but once we step back inside, it will be clear."

"But I haven't even done anything."

"Do you know how long it's been? My body's been pent up for years and now—"

Caryn stared at him stunned. "You mean all this time you haven't...?"

"Not with you," he clarified with a quick grin of mischief. "That's the difference and I think we should talk about something else or I'm going to stay happy longer than we both want."

"What should we do?"

"First I suggest you stop looking down like that."

Caryn snapped her head up. "Yes, right."

"And now let me go, just don't move away."

She took a step back and narrowed her eyes. "Are you sure you're not teasing me?"

"I swear." He shoved his hands in his pockets.

Her eyes widened. "What are you doing?"

He yanked his hands out. "Nothing. What kind of guy do you take me for?"

She folded her arms. "The kind of guy who forces me to stand out here like a ninny because he's 'happy to see me'."

Adrian rubbed his jaw. "Don't worry, I'm getting less happy by the minute."

"Good," she said, searching for another way to needle him. "Because you should encourage Ken to stop smoking. And I didn't want to say anything, but did you know your coat doesn't really fit your trousers? The color is a shade off as well as the cut."

He turned. "Okay, we can go back inside now."

"Great," Caryn said, sashaying in front of him,

pleased her nagging worked. She threw a naughty grin over her shoulder. "I'll tell you the color of my new panties later," she said.

But Adrian wasn't in the mood to wait and they never made it back to the ballroom.

CHAPTER TWENTY-TWO

Hazel looked at her son, trying to ignore the dark fire in his gaze as they sat across from each other in her dining room. The late afternoon sun seemed too scared to enter the room, leaving them in a dim haze, dulling the sight of her glass table and pastel colored centerpiece of fake fruits. "I know I'm beautiful," she said after a long moment, "but you don't have to keep staring at me like that."

He blinked.

"I was protecting you."

He ran his finger along the table.

"What did Monica tell you?"

He drummed his fingers.

"I'm talking to you," Hazel said losing patience. "At least say something."

He glanced away. "Is the piano still out of tune?"

She looked at the upright piano in the family room. "I don't know."

He stood up, sitting down on the bench and hit a key. "Adrian—"

"Yes, it's still out of tune. Why even keep it if you're not going to care for it?"

"You're the only one who played it."

He struck a chord. "It sounds awful."

"It doesn't sound that bad to me."

He closed the lid. "You shouldn't have interfered."

Hazel rubbed her hands under the table, glad he was ready to talk. "I thought it was best."

He spun around. "For who? For me? Did you once think about how you made her feel? What did you say to her?"

"Don't stand up for her. She should have told you the truth about her mother."

He rested back against the piano. "It wouldn't have made a difference."

"It should."

"So you told her to leave me?"

"I told her to set you free."

"I—"

"Do you remember the box?"

He turned back to the piano and lifted the lid.

Hazel knew he was shutting her out, but she wouldn't let him succeed. "I do, because that's where we found you. Malnourished, dehydrated inside of a wooden box where my sister kept you. I went through one month of hell because my sister kidnapped my son—my baby—and wanted him for herself. Your father and I struggled to get our little boy back to health, stopping him from eating until he was sick, keeping the light on in his room because darkness scared him, but what scared him more was being locked in a room or any small spaces."

Adrian tapped his finger along the piano keys. "That has nothing to do with Caryn."

"I know what it's like to have a family member you constantly have to watch and worry about. Although we didn't press formal charges, we had to make arrangements for someone to look after her. I know how it can strain one's health and marriage. There were so many times your father and I fought because of my sister. Love can lead to resentment. I didn't keep you safe once, I'll never let that happen again."

He stood and returned to the table. "Mom, what happened to me wasn't your fault." He gathered her hands in his then gently said, "When will you forgive yourself?"

Tears choked her voice. "I don't think I can."

"Remember when I couldn't go to sleep how you'd sing 'Yellow Bird'?"

She stiffened and pulled her hands free. "I never sang you that song. She did."

He frowned. "Are you sure?"

"I'm certain." She sighed. "But I can't blame you for not remembering correctly, you were only a child."

"Exactly, and I'm a man now. You don't have to worry about me."

She reached up and touched his cheek. "You don't know what you're doing."

"Yes, I do."

"Then give it some time. You don't need to rush things."

"I've waited eight years."

Hazel let her hand fall in defeat. "No matter what I say, you're still determined to marry her?"

He nodded.

"Then do one thing for me first."

"What?"

"Tell her to take you to her mother's house."

CHAPTER TWENTY-THREE

He should confront her.

Adrian stood in front of Ken's apartment door, knowing he should be talking to Caryn, but he wasn't ready yet. It had been two weeks since the spring gala and their time together had been like heaven to him. As spring gave way to summer, they'd spent every moment they could together—discussing the simple wedding ceremony they'd have, even though they still hadn't pinned down a date; making arrangements around his apartment for when she moved in.

She'd surprised him one evening when he'd come home and found her laying on her side on top of his piano wearing a gold colored teddy and thigh-high lace stockings.

"Play something for me," she'd said in a low purr.

He sauntered over to her in measured steps as if afraid if he moved too fast the dream would disappear. Caryn had never been this playful before. In front of him was a whole new woman. Yes, that was the difference. She was a confident, sexy woman who knew the power of her body and his weakness for it. And that knowledge didn't bother him a bit. Because the years had also taught him a few things.

He slid his hand up her leg, his voice deepening. "I'd rather play you."

"I'm a complicated instrument."

"Any instrument can be mastered."

She sat up. "It takes practice."

He pulled her towards him. "I plan to start now," he said then swept her into his arms. And he'd been practicing every day since.

"Thank you for forgiving me," she'd told him one evening after they'd finished a bath together and lay in bed.

"You've already said that."

"I can't say it enough."

But he didn't just want her to be grateful. He wanted her to know how much it was destiny. That Halloween night hadn't been a mistake, it had been one of true magic. But not by a spell that could be broken. It was something stronger than that. A love that knew no bounds, that couldn't be battered by time. One day he wanted her to surrender to the fact that she'd tried to run from something they both couldn't escape.

His mother and her aunt had tried to separate them and failed. He remembered telling her there was no need to apologize anymore and holding her ringed hand in his wanting to say, 'don't let anyone steal you away from me again. Trust me no matter what,' but since words seemed inadequate, he just held her close.

When they weren't in bed, they were enjoying other adventures.

Last weekend he and Caryn had even gone indoor rock climbing, although Caryn had initially been terrified. He'd made the suggestion just to tease her, but she'd surprised him by saying yes.

With his coaxing and support she'd made it to the top and cheered when she reached it. The look on her face still made him smile. And when she was on the ground again, she'd hugged him and said, "I'm so glad I did this with you," making him suddenly eager to make more memories with her to make up for the time lost.

He hadn't told her about the conversation he'd had with his mother. He hadn't asked her to show him her mother's place. Part of him wanted her to volunteer, but she didn't and that worried him and made him wonder if he could lose her again.

If his mother had been able to make her doubt him once, could she convince her again?

But what troubled him most was why. Why hadn't she told him the full truth? Why had she still not told him? What was she afraid of? Why didn't she trust him?

He needed to sort out his thoughts, which was why he'd told Caryn he'd be busy the next couple of days, and ended up on a Saturday afternoon on his best friend's doorstep.

"Still in the mood to break my fingers?" Ken said when he opened the door.

In the background Adrian heard a Portuguese hip

hop song playing, smelled the sweet scent of coconuts and sugar, and noticed a red high heel shoe under a glass side table in the foyer. "You have company?"

Ken looked down and swore, grabbing the shoe. "How did I miss that? She's going to want to come back."

"And you don't want that?" Adrian said, stepping inside.

Ken held the shoe by it's heel and spun it around. "This woman is scary."

Adrian walked to the living room. "I told you one nighters are dangerous."

Ken grabbed a remote and turned the music off. "She wasn't. I'd been eying her for a while, but she's a little too wild for me."

Adrian walked towards the coconut smell, which led him to the kitchen. "What are you working on?" he asked, noticing the tray of coconut covered cookies, cooling on a tray.

Ken couldn't stop a smile. "I've outdone myself." He pointed then ducked his head and feigned a look of humility. "Come on. Ask me how good these are."

Adrian leaned against the counter. "How good are they?"

Ken stood to his full height and held up his hands as if he expected applause. "These are smack-your-mama good."

Adrian picked one up and took a bite. Soft, chewy sweetness melted in his mouth. He groaned and closed his eyes. "Sorry Mom, but I'm going to have to hurt you." He looked at his friend, gave him a high-five, and in an instant any residual bad feelings fell away.

Adrian grabbed two more cookies then took a seat in the living room. "When did you start smoking again?"

"Why?" Ken asked, setting two small bottles of apple juice on the coffee table.

"Caryn wants me to ask you to quit."

Ken grinned, sitting in front of him. "I did it to tick her off."

"And where did you get the smokes?"

"Swiped them off a guy who didn't need them for a while. What?" Ken said when Adrian lifted his brows in shock. "He didn't notice and I gave them right back."

Adrian shook his head. "You're not that cool, try again."

"Okay. I knew she'd come looking for me, so I asked a friend."

He nodded. "That's better."

Ken watched Adrian finish another cookie, then said, "So, aside from enjoying the taste of my genius, what brings you here?"

Adrian sat back and rested his hand on the back of the couch. "It's my mom."

Ken's good humor died, his brown gaze shifting to concern. "There's something wrong with her?"

"No, I talked to her and... My mom knew about..." He ran a hand down his face, searching for the right words. "She talked to Caryn before the wedding and convinced her not to marry me."

Ken swore; Adrian nodded.

"Why?" Ken asked.

"Something to do with Caryn's mother."

Ken winced then shook his hand as if he'd touched

something hot. "Ooh a woman with mother issues. That's bad. Maybe your mother's right."

"About what?'

"We all know mother-in-laws can be hellish, but a crazy mother in law? That's an entire new dimension."

The doorbell rang. Ken jumped up and checked the peephole. "Damn it's her."

"Red shoe?"

"Yeah." He made an impatient motion with his hand. "Toss it to me."

Adrian threw the shoe at him. "Want me to disappear?"

"No, this won't take long." He opened the door, but not wide enough for Adrian to see who the young woman was. "Hi," he said and the young woman replied so low that Adrian couldn't hear. "Yeah, you left this... No, nothing happened... Uh...right. Of course. Sure. Bye." He closed the door.

"I thought you—" Adrian stopped when Ken pressed a finger to his lips. He rested his head against the door as if listening for something then pushed himself away. "Go on," he said.

Adrian glanced at the door. "You told her nothing happened."

Ken sat down, running a hand through his hair. "She doesn't remember anything. I don't want her to feel bad."

"But you—"

He held up his hands in surrender. "I didn't take advantage of her."

"You said she was scary."

"Yes, she was." He leaned forward, resting his elbows

on his knees. "She comes on to me, right? And I'm thinking *Obrigado, Deus*, I'm going to get lucky tonight. We have fun. Drink a little, okay more than a little, make out and I'm ready to slide to home base when she asks me, 'Do you like doggy style?' and I'm like 'Sure' and then you know what she does?"

Adrian folded his arms. "Asks for a dog collar?"

"No, worse. She strips down naked, gets down on all fours and starts howling like she's a wolf or something. And she starts rubbing her head against my leg, asking me to stroke her."

"And you do?"

"Sure, if that turns her on, I'm fine with it, but then she scratches me, jumps on top of me and passes out."

"You're right," Adrian said with a laugh. "She's scary. Fortunately, Caryn isn't."

Ken waved his finger in warning. "But her mother may be."

"I met her mother at the wedding. She seemed all right."

"So did this girl. You never know until you get people behind closed doors. You've got to find out what's got your mother so worried. Caryn is hiding something big about her mother. You love her, right?"

"Of course."

Ken held out his hands. "If you want to cook in the kitchen, you can't be afraid of the flames."

CHAPTER TWENTY-FOUR

Caryn looked down at the image of an emaciated three year old with sad brown eyes.

"His mother wanted you to see this again," her aunt said. "In case you've forgotten."

She pushed the picture back across her office table. Her office was located in the walk-out basement of her townhouse and was already considering keeping it while renting the upstairs living area when she moved in with Adrian. At first she'd been pleased to have her aunt stop by for lunch so that she could share her plans, until her aunt made clear the true reason why she'd wanted to see her.

Barbara tapped the photo. "Doesn't this boy have a right to a happy future?"

"He's happy with me." Although Adrian had been busier than usual over the past several days, Caryn brushed aside her concern.

"For how long?" her aunt pressed. "He's not strong.

He still fears enclosed spaces. You need a strong, stable man you can depend on. You're two broken people. How can you hope to have a healthy relationship for years to come? You grew up in a garbage heap and he was kidnapped and left in a box. You both don't have the tools to recognize what normal really is."

"Yes we do."

"It isn't normal to fall in love with someone after one kiss. It isn't normal to agree to marry only after a few months. It isn't normal to see someone eight years later and rush into each other's arms as if nothing has happened. And forgive me for being so plain, but I don't care how good the sex is, you're both not thinking with the right organ. You're both damaged—"

Caryn's brows shot up. "Damaged?"

"That was the wrong choice of words."

"But that's how you feel."

Barbara glanced at one of the framed testimonials from one of Caryn's satisfied customers that decorated the wall. "I'll be honest, I expected more from you. Considering his upbringing, his rash behavior is to be expected, but you..." She turned to her. "Are you going to throw away all that I've taught you?"

"No, my eyes are wide open."

"You're more fragile than you think, and need someone whose background—"

"Is better than mine, right? Because my history is so tainted and foul I need someone with a sterling background to clean it."

"What will he do when your mother has another major episode? What about your sister? Do you know what the future holds for her? What will you do if the stress of your family causes him to leave you with a child or two to raise?"

"I'm not my mother."

"It's in our lowest moments when we face our true selves. Neither of you have had to face a crisis together. Everything may seem so right now, but he's not the only man out there for you."

"Yes, he is."

"You say you're not like your mother, then why are you being selfish like her? Why are you considering no one else's feelings but your own?"

"Is it wrong for me to be happy?"

"At what price? He doesn't need you. Look at what he became without you in his life. Do you really think he could have achieved all this success if you'd gotten married all those years ago? I don't mean to be cruel, but you need him more than he could ever need you. You're not the only woman alive who can make him happy. You knew that years ago and you must remember it now." She held up the photograph. "When you hold on too tight to something you can squeeze the life out of it. If nothing else, your mother must have taught you that." Barbara set the photo on the table and slide it in front of Caryn again. "If you truly love him, you will let him go."

LET GO. *Let go. Let go.* The words echoed in her mind even as she lay in Adrian's arms. Was she being selfish? Was she being arrogant? She'd held her resolve until her aunt left. Then stared at the picture of the little boy Adrian had been, and burst into tears just as she had years ago when she'd first seen it. He had suffered and she never wanted him to suffer again, but she didn't want to let go. She wanted them to stay together.

"What are you hiding from me?" Adrian said, his voice a low rumble in his chest.

A shiver of panic raced through her. Why would he ask that? "Nothing. Why would I be hiding anything?"

He fell silent then said, "I'm going to ask you again. What are you hiding from me?" When she didn't reply he said, "Why didn't you tell me you spoke to my mother the day before the wedding? You didn't mention that in your note."

How had he found out? "She wasn't the one who convinced me."

"How about your aunt?"

She flattened her hand against his chest. "If you want to blame someone blame me."

"Not the mental illness?"

Caryn froze. "What are you talking about?"

"Monica said it runs in your family."

How much did he know? "Yes, a form of it does."

"And you didn't want to tell me this?"

"No."

"Why not?"

"Everything happened so fast."

"That was then. How about now?"

Her throat turned dry, she couldn't read his tone. "I didn't want it to get in the way."

Her phone rang. She felt him laugh. "Saved by the bell again."

Caryn picked up her phone, but instead of a sense of relief she felt a growing dread. "Roland, can I—"

"I can't get a hold of Mom. Can you go and check on her?"

Caryn checked the time. "Fine, tomorrow I'll—"

"You need to go right now. Something isn't right. I would do it, but you're closer."

"She's probably fine and doesn't want to pick up the phone."

"It's been three days."

Damn. "Okay." She hung up.

"What is it?" Adrian asked, searching her face.

Caryn stood and started to change, the sense of looming dread thickening. "I have to go check in on my mom. My brother's worried."

"I'll drive you there."

"No, you don't have to. I—"

His cutting glance stopped her words. "I think it's time I see the truth."

CHAPTER TWENTY-FIVE

Caryn looked at the two-story house then turned away as Adrian parked his car in the driveway. "She's alright, I'm sure she's all right. I shouldn't have to do this."

He shut off the engine. "What's wrong?"

"Everything will be fine. Why did he have to worry so much?" She closed her eyes and saw piles of debris, items stacked to the ceiling. She couldn't breathe. She saw little Brandon hanging by a rope in his bedroom and...

"Caryn," Adrian said, her name a sharp command.

She opened her eyes.

"What happened in that house?"

Too much. It was all too much. Too much stuff, too much need, too little love. "I'm sorry I asked you to come."

"You didn't ask me. You didn't have a choice. You still don't." He unbuckled his seatbelt.

She grabbed his arm before he could open the door.

"I don't want you to see."

"What?"

"If you go in there, it will end things between us."

He shook his head. "No, it won't."

"You'll see it's all a lie. I'm a lie."

"I doubt that." He opened the car door and got out.

Caryn followed. "You're going to see what I could become. Maybe who I am deep down."

He closed the car door and locked it. "Caryn—"

"You'll meet my mother."

"I met her at the wedding."

"No, you didn't meet the real her. She looks normal but...that house." Caryn looked at the seemingly harmless structure noticing the new white rose bushes which joined the purple azaleas and pink peonies along the trim. "It's filled with trash. It's stacked to the ceiling with stuff. And she won't notice. She'll have cleared a path for you and you'll have to pretend that you're not afraid that one of the piles won't dislodge and topple on you. And you'll ignore the dust and the cobwebs. But you won't be able to, because to you it will be a small crowded space like a tomb. If you could look through the windows, I'd let you, but you can't. So this has to be as far as you go. Stay here." She walked up to the front door.

He followed her. "No."

"You can't come in."

"I have to see."

"You don't like small places and—"

"I'll be fine. Let's go."

"Adrian."

"You can fight me, but you'll still lose."

Caryn silently swore then knocked on the door and rang the doorbell. She waited a few minutes, knowing it would take her mother that long to reach the front door, but when nothing happened she pulled out her key and opened the door as wide as she could. At least her mother hadn't completely blocked the entryway as many hoarders did, but she still could barely squeeze through. Caryn turned to Adrian in one last desperate attempt to keep him out. "You see this? This is the cleanliest part. So just peek through, you don't need to come in. Stay here."

"You think you're mother's hurt, right?"

"It's possible."

"And you want me to stay out here and do nothing?"

"Yes, just give me a few minutes."

His flat gaze made it clear he planned to do nothing of the sort.

She sighed then walked further inside. "Follow closely behind me, don't step anywhere I don't. Don't touch anything either, okay?"

He nodded.

Caryn climbed over the pile of clothes, old wrapping and newspapers, then crawled into another room. "Mom?" When she didn't hear a reply she went further inside the maze. She turned to Adrian, trying not to notice how his breathing had become more labored, or the sheen of sweat glistening on his forehead. "You've seen more than enough. Go back."

He swallowed, wiping his forehead. "I won't leave you," he said through gritted teeth. "I'll help you find her."

Caryn walked up the stairs and called her mother's

name again. "Mom." She started to grow panicked as she entered several rooms and saw nothing, trying to assess each mountain of stuff to see if anything had shifted out of place. Could her mother be under it? Then she heard a noise, the sound of water. She opened the bathroom door and found her mother lazing in the bathtub. She stared at her stunned. Her mother hadn't taken a bath in years. She'd never had the room.

Her mother looked up at her and screamed, covering herself. "What are you doing!"

"I thought something was wrong," Caryn said, angered that she'd been worried for nothing.

"What could be wrong?"

"Roland's been trying to reach you."

"I must have turned the phone off. I was working on cleaning things up." She gestured to the room, which could pass for a linen closet with all the towels, sheets and bedding that cluttered it. "Aren't you impressed? I couldn't take a bath before and I wanted to treat myself. There's no reason to worry about me."

The sound of a loud crash interrupted Caryn's reply.

"What was that?" her mother demanded, grabbing a robe.

Caryn felt her heart leap into her throat. *Adrian.* She'd forgotten about him. She scrambled out of the room calling his name. "Adrian!" She searched the top floor then made her way downstairs to the main floor calling his name until her voice grew hoarse.

She didn't get a reply, then stopped when she saw one of the towers gone, scattered on the ground.

Beneath it she saw a hand.

CHAPTER TWENTY-SIX

She began to dig. "Mom! Help me please." He was being crushed to death. Maybe he already was...no she wouldn't believe it. She had to reach him; she had to get him out.

"Stop doing that," her mother snapped. "You're making it worse. Look, my porcelain doll," her voice dropped to a whimper, "it got broken."

"Mom, you need to focus."

"Don't shout at me."

Caryn held out her mobile phone. "Call 911."

Her mother stared down at the object as if it were foreign to her. "Why?"

Caryn continued to dig. "We need the fire department."

"I don't want them in my house."

"Mom, we can't—"

"This is all your fault. You shouldn't have brought a stranger into my house."

Caryn heard a moan, saw a finger flicker. "Stay still, Adrian," she said in a soothing tone. "We'll get you out. Mom, call the police. Now!"

Her mother reached down and started to move items. "No, we can do this ourselves."

"You're making it worse."

"No, I'm not. I'm helping you."

Caryn shook her mobile at her. "Call them."

Her mother glanced down at her robe. "I'm not dressed for visitors."

"Mom! Call 911."

"No, they'll force me out of my home. They tried to last time—"

Caryn glared at her, her tone tinged with acid. "Call them now, or I swear I'll smash everything I see."

Her mother took her mobile phone and started to dial.

Caryn heard Adrian moan again. She bent down and saw a small pocket where some air could reach him. "Help is coming."

"I can't breathe."

"Yes, you can. I'm here. We'll get you out." He couldn't panic; that would make things worse. She took his hand and held it between hers. His beautiful large hand. A hand that had caressed her cheek and slid a ring of promise on her finger. She held his hand, wishing she had the strength to pull him free. "They're coming."

"I'm sorry."

"No, don't speak. You didn't do anything wrong." She felt his grip growing weak and she fought to push away the image of the three year old with the sad brown eyes who'd been trapped in the box; her aunt's harsh words, *You need him more than he could ever need you*; her friend's accusation that she was a thinking with her heart instead of her head. She held his hand, rigidly holding back tears and the wave of misery that threatened to consume her. "They're coming. Oh they're here," she lied. "I think I hear them outside. It will take some time for them to organize how to free you, so just be patient. They have to be careful, but don't worry, they'll get to you and you'll soon be free." And as she continued to hold his hand, she knew that she would eventually have to let him go.

CHAPTER TWENTY-SEVEN

"You nearly killed my son."

Monica held her mother back, afraid she would attack Caryn when she saw her in the waiting room. "Mom—"

"I'm sorry," Caryn said, her face a mask of misery. "It was an accident."

Hazel bared her teeth. "I want you to stay away from my family. You should have stayed away when I told you to." She motioned down the corridor. "My son has a punctured lung, a broken clavicle and possibly a fractured skull. Why did you have to take him inside that house of horrors? What did you have to prove?"

"I'm truly sorry."

Hazel lowered her voice. "Show me that you mean it and get out of my sight."

Caryn balled her hands into fists, took a deep breath, then nodded. "Okay," she said then left.

"Mom, she's worried as much as we are."

Hazel fell into a chair, tears blinding her. "You keep that woman away from my son."

Monica rested her arm around her shoulders. "He's going to want to see her."

"Then lie. Tell him that she ran away again, she did it before. He'll believe you."

"He's hurting enough, Mom. I can't hurt him like that again."

Hazel squeezed her eyes shut. "I'm glad your father isn't here to see this. To see his son's greatest fear of being buried alive come true."

"But he survived it."

Hazel glared at her daughter. "It shouldn't have happened. He shouldn't have been there."

"I thought you wanted him to see Caryn's mother's house. Her aunt told us it was bad."

Hazel pulled away from her, outraged. "Are you blaming me for this?"

"No, I'm just..." Monica sighed and shook her head. "It was an accident."

"That woman should have looked out for him. You and Adrian are my heart. I'll guard you with my life. With every breath of my body. She will never get close to him again."

MONICA STOOD by her brother's hospital bed wondering how much time she had before her mother returned. To everyone's relief, he'd pulled through surgery to repair his broken clavicle and was healing well, but she hadn't had a moment alone with him, as they performed various tests to rule out any possible brain injuries, and was desperate to tell him what she'd seen.

He seemed just as eager to talk to her because the moment their mother left to get something from the cafeteria, his gaze sharpened and he said, "Where's Caryn?"

"Mom, won't let her see you."

"What do you mean? Why not?"

"She blames her."

He struggled to sit up. "She's keeping Caryn away from me?"

"Don't get upset," Monica said, gently adjusting the bed. "She's trying to protect you. She's...she's frightened right now and..."

His tone hardened. "I don't care."

"You should have seen her face. She'd thought she'd lost you."

"How long have I been here?"

"You can't leave yet."

"I have to see Caryn."

"If anything happens to you, mother will blame Caryn even more. Do you want that?"

"I need to see her."

"I can talk to her for you."

He narrowed his eyes. "Why should I trust you?"

She sent a nervous glance towards the door. "Because I saw how much Caryn loves you. I didn't believe it at first, until I saw her with Mom. What Mom said to her... I know she didn't mean to be so cruel, but she was, and Caryn just took it. And I thought she'd walked away, but then I saw her waiting in another part of the hospital and... I don't know... there was something about her expression and her stance that made me know she wasn't going to leave your side no matter what Mom said, and part of me felt glad.

"Then I saw her aunt approach her and I overheard them talking and Caryn was explaining what happened, and I thought her aunt would comfort her because Caryn looked really upset, but instead she said, 'See? I told you you were dangerous,' and walked away. Caryn slid to the ground and cried." Monica hugged herself. "I wanted to go to her, but I didn't know what to say. That's when she looked up and saw me. She jumped up and raced down the hall."

Adrian swore. "And you haven't seen her since?"

Monica let her hands fall. "No."

Adrian closed his eyes and took a deep, steadying breath. "I want to see her."

"I told you Mom will have a fit."

He opened his eyes. "No, I want to see her aunt."

"She probably won't come."

Anger blazed in his gaze. "She'll come."

"How do you know?"

"Because I'll tell her what she wants to hear. That I'm going to let Caryn go."

CHAPTER TWENTY-EIGHT

Barbara didn't have much use for hospitals. She was glad her dear Murray had died at home. But after receiving the message she'd gotten from Adrian's sister, she was starting to see the building in a new light and felt almost giddy with joy. At last her niece would be free of this man's hold. He wouldn't take Caryn from her and she'd find the right man suitable for her.

Barbara walked into the private hospital room and looked at the man in the bed. He was a very handsome man, even with the bandages, and rich, which was a nice bonus. Pity he was such a terrible prospect for marriage. She plastered on a bright smile. "I'm glad to see you're much better." She took a seat. "Caryn's been in a tizzy, but then you've always had that rather unhealthy affect on her."

Adrian's brows drew together. "I'd argue that your influence is the one that's unhealthy."

Barbara crossed her legs and shrugged. "We can agree to disagree."

"No, we can agree on this much. You have complete sway over her mind, while I have sway over her heart. Should we find out and see which one will dominate?"

Barbara toyed with her necklace, amused. Right now he was as helpless as a lamb. "You can't beat me. I know how to push all her buttons."

Adrian shook his head. "I don't intend to beat you, because I don't want to fight. I love her too much to rip her into two just to satisfy my own ego."

"Does that mean you surrender?"

"I won't see her hurt because of me."

A sly grin touched Barbara's mouth. "You're a romantic." She stood up and bent over a bouquet of flowers. "I can't stand romantics. Foolish dreamers who force the rest of us to clean up their messes." She turned to him. "My sister is a romantic, and Caryn could be too, if I let her. But I won't let it happen." She leaned against the windowsill. "So it's agreed that you'll no longer pursue her?"

"Only on one condition. If she comes to me, you won't interfere."

"You sound confident that she will, but I know for certain that she won't. And do you know why? Because once I leave here I'll tell her that I saw you. No, I won't share what we discussed, I'll just describe the pallor of your skin, the IV drip in your arm. Every chance I get, I'll remind her that she's the reason you're here."

His jaw twitched. "It wasn't her fault."

Barbara approached his bed. "I'll also remind her that

if it hadn't been for you, her mother's secret wouldn't have been revealed."

His tone sharpened. "What does that have to do with anything?'

"Oh yes, you haven't heard. Caryn has two weeks to clean up her mother's entire property or it will be condemned and she'll be homeless. I'm sure Caryn has you to thank for that. And if that isn't enough, there are her nightmares. She's already told me how when she closes her eyes she sees your hand sticking out of the rubble. The helplessness and guilt she feels. I'll continue to stoke those fires until she runs far away from you."

Adrian looked at her perplexed. "You hate me that much?"

"Yes," Barbara hissed, gripping the rails of his bed. "I hate the joy that you put on her face. The joy that I used to put there. She's mine and she still needs me, but you're confusing her."

He sent a significant look at her hands. "You can't hold onto her forever."

"Neither can you."

"She loves me."

Barbara picked up her handbag. "I know." She headed for the door, pleased the meeting had been successful. "That's what I'm counting on."

CHAPTER TWENTY-NINE

Adrian watched Barbara leave, regret ripping his heart in two. He'd made a mistake. He'd underestimated her. They all had. Caryn's mother wasn't the true threat, her aunt was. She hid her madness well, it was borderline, but he'd seen it in her gaze. That too bright gaze of unflinching certainty in a reality that didn't exist. A reality that said she was judge and jury over Caryn's life.

Caryn lived in a life of two extremes—her mother suffered from too little control while her aunt suffered from too much. But both were about possession. He knew Barbara would destroy Caryn before releasing her. He'd entered a battle he couldn't win. He hadn't calculated how much she wanted to keep Caryn away from him, that she'd stoop to lying to her, to hurting her. That she'd use Caryn's weakness to manipulate her. If he told Caryn what he knew he doubted Caryn would believe him. She loved her aunt too much and depended on her.

He rested his head back on the pillow, feeling the

shame of his cowardice. If he hadn't panicked and tried to get out of the house so quickly, he wouldn't have dislodged the stack of items.

What if that's what Caryn would remember? Her aunt wouldn't need to persuade her at all if she remembered how she'd gone to rescue her mother and had ended up rescuing him instead. What kind of a husband would he be?

He'd thought he'd conquered his fear. He could ride elevators now; he could even take short trips on the metro. But that house. God...that *house*. It felt almost alive, as if it were closing in on him.

The first moment he stepped inside he wanted to run back out again. He'd put on a mask of calm so that Caryn could focus on her mother and not worry about him. But the deeper they got into the house—the piles of clothes, the boxes, the papers—he felt his breathing quicken, felt the tingling of his skin. He couldn't see any floors or windows. He didn't know where to rest his eyes. What room was he in? They all looked alike. The sudden sight of the stairs had startled him. He'd forgotten they were in a house that it was large enough to have two levels. They'd climbed the stairs, his feet slipping on old newspapers, and he'd felt his vision grow blurry, sweat causing his shirt to cling to his back.

Her mother, he had to focus on finding Caryn's mother. When she finally did, the relief in him nearly made him faint. He could escape now. And that had been his sole purpose—to get out. He had to get out.

But he couldn't find his way. He went down the stairs but suddenly felt lost in a labyrinth. A labyrinth that seemed to grow smaller and smaller with each step. He felt as if the tunnels between the boxes were moving in closer and closer. He grabbed the front of his shirt, the collar feeling too tight, the room too warm. It was too warm because there were no windows. Why couldn't he find any windows? Where was the door? Didn't the place have a back door? He needed to find a door. A door to get out. He must get out.

He stumbled forward then saw a door and pulled. But too late he learned it wasn't a route of escape; it was another chamber of horrors. A closet filled to the brim, with stuff, and like a live monster, it swayed. He quickly tried to close the door, but not soon enough. Items fell forward and he stumbled back to protect his head. That's when the avalanche happened.

Within seconds he was buried. He could feel the weight of the items pressing him into the ground, darkness surrounding him, and there was no way out. He kept his hand outstretched; it was the only part of his body he could move. He had a small pocket of air, due to one small box that kept the rest of the pile from completely crushing him. But it didn't matter.

He was dying.

Slowly.

His body couldn't register pain, just fear. Fear that this would be his final moment. Fear that no one would find him. He couldn't scream. Just like then. Alone in the box. In the dark. It had been so hot. Why was it so hot?

You'll be safe here, the voice, he now knew as his aunt, had said.

But he didn't feel safe. He felt scared. He didn't like

being there. He wanted his Mommy and Daddy. Why did his aunt keep him there? She said she was keeping him away from monsters, but he saw monsters in the box. He wanted to get out. Out! But when he cried out she got angry and banged on the box.

Only the bird made her stop. She liked the sound of the bird and soon he listened for the bird too. The bird was his friend. His only companion. It would chirp. And he imagined being a bird himself and flying away like the song she sang 'Yellow Bird.'

Soon he felt himself drifting away, free from every-thing, soaring to the sky. Then he heard Caryn's voice and felt her hand.

If he could have moved, he would have pulled his hand away. He didn't want her to see him like this. He didn't want her to worry about him. He didn't want to be a burden to her. If he'd followed closely to the path she'd shown him, this wouldn't have happened.

But once she touched him, he selfishly took hold. She was his life, his breath. His little bird outside of the box that never left him. That called to him. He registered pain and shame, but still she was his strength. But breathing was still hard. And waves of panic still threat-ened to consume him.

He listened to her voice. And before he lost consciousness he prayed, *My love. My love. Don't leave me.*

Adrian stared up at the ceiling of the hospital room. But she had left him. He hadn't gotten a chance to explain, and he knew her aunt would plant false thoughts in her mind.

"So how did it go?" his sister asked, coming into the room.

"I ruined it."

"How?"

He told her about his conversation with Barbara.

Monica fell into a chair and sighed. "Did you make an agreement in blood? Tell her you changed your mind."

"It's not about me, it's what she can do to Caryn. She'll hurt her if I don't stay away. Plus, there's a chance Caryn blames me for what happened to her mother. It's a mess."

"Well she's an organizer, now it's her chance to prove herself."

Adrian frowned. "Prove herself?"

Monica nodded. "Everybody knows how much you love her, but how much does she love you?"

CHAPTER THIRTY

She couldn't save her.

Caryn lay on her couch after another day of trying to get her mother's house up to code feeling beaten and worn. Her mother's words still echoed. "I hate you. Leave me alone! This is all your fault!"

Her brother walked away many times fed up with the abuse, her sister left in tears, but Caryn soldiered on as best she could. Despite her mother taking items out of the junk truck or shoving her away when Caryn took items to be donated, determined to supervise every item that would leave the house. She didn't seem to realize the urgency. At times she just sat in the living room, smoothing out wrapping paper as if they were printed gold.

"Let them take the house," her brother had said after one shouting match.

"Then what would we do with her?"

"Hell if I know."

She'd gotten a small reprieve when she'd pulled some strings and gotten an extension.

But it was still an uphill battle. And she didn't want to be alone. She wanted to be with Adrian. She wanted to bury her head in his chest and hold him tight. She wanted her mother to disappear from her life. Adrian had nearly been killed because she'd left him alone. She should have led him out. How could she have been so careless with something so precious?

She'd stayed away from visiting him, not because his mother asked her to, or even because her aunt continued to remind her where she placed blame. She stayed away because she wanted him to heal. What would he think of her now? Every time he looked at her face, would he remember that day? Her aunt Barbara had told her that he looked awful, traumatized, that they had him on anti-anxiety medicines. Had she really pushed him back that far? She needed to give him space to get over the trauma.

Plus she had to deal with the end of her sister's marriage. Ella had called her and told her that Louis had moved out and served her papers. Happy endings weren't in the cards for them.

Caryn closed her eyes. She just wanted to sleep. A knock on the door interrupted her plans. She softly swore then got up to answer it, expecting to see Terri who'd been helping her through the clean up. Instead she saw Rania. "I think it's time you stopped feeling sorry for yourself," she said.

Caryn shook her head and returned to the couch. "I don't need this right now."

"I'm exactly what you need. Isn't it time you stopped running away from him?"

"In case you haven't noticed, I haven't done anything."

"Doing nothing is the same thing as doing something. If you let water leak through your roof and don't patch it up, you're still letting water leak through your roof. Do you want to see him?"

Yes. "I can't see him yet."

"Why not?"

"His mother—"

"I'm not asking about his mother, I'm asking about him. Do you want to see him?"

"I can't—"

"This is not a hard question."

Caryn threw up her hands, exasperated. "Yes."

"Then go see him."

"You don't understand. His mother—"

"Does he live with his mother?"

"No."

"Then what's stopping you?"

Caryn waved her hands. "I'm not doing this." She went to her bedroom then returned carrying the box from The Black Stockings Society. "You can take this back. I'll pay whatever penalty."

Rania barely glanced at the box, her gaze fixated on Caryn's face. "Giving up things is easy for you, isn't it?"

Caryn's eyebrows shot up. "You think this is easy?"

"For you? Yes. Letting go is easier than holding on."

"That's not true."

"Then why won't you see him?"

"I'm afraid to."

"Why?"

She gripped her hands into fists. "Because then I won't want to let him go."

"So?"

"And I'll want to hold onto him as tightly as...as tightly as..."

"Your mother holds onto to her things?" Rania finished.

"Yes," she said in a raw whisper.

"It's not the same. Holding onto something out of love is not the same as holding onto something you want to possess. You've become so afraid of holding onto anything you've not allowed yourself to see the difference."

"What about that saying that if you love something you let it go? My aunt—"

"Is not always right. She saved you once. She gave you a place to stay, but you don't owe her your life for that. It's okay to disappoint her."

"She's helped me so much and—"

"Her disapproval hurts?"

Caryn nodded.

"Has she ever told you how proud she is of you?"

Caryn stared at her surprised. She'd never thought of that, but her aunt rarely praised her. She was usually critical. *You're fragile. You're damage. Don't be like your mother.*

Rania saw the look of realization and nodded. "Yes,

that's how she's kept you close. It's time you broke free from caring about what she thinks of you."

Caryn covered her eyes as the pedestal she'd put under her aunt slowly crumbled. She'd wanted to be like her. Did that make her crazy too? "I've done everything wrong."

"No, you haven't. When Adrian was buried, what did you do?"

"I talked to him and tried to get him out."

"And when you couldn't, what did you do?"

She searched her memory. "I held his hand."

"Why?"

"Because I wanted him to know I was there."

"Did you hold it the entire time?"

"Yes, until the firefighters could reach him."

"Why didn't you let go?"

"What?"

Rania lifted a brow. "If you truly loved him, shouldn't you have let go?"

"No, he needed me."

"So you held on."

"Yes, of course."

"Do you see the difference now? Letting go of something is not the same as abandoning it. Running away, pushing away, building up walls is not letting go, that's turning your back. There are things you have to hold onto, that you have to fight for, that you have to claim as yours. You're not your mother nor your aunt, or even your sister. Live the life you were meant to live. There is nothing wrong with holding onto the man you love no matter who it hurts, because you deserve to be loved by him."

"But what if—"

Rania shook her head. "We don't deal in 'what ifs'. You have one special pair of stockings left. I think you know how to use them."

CHAPTER THIRTY-ONE

Adrian paid the driver, who'd taken him to the Lucky Stars restaurant, wondering what carnage he'd find in the kitchen. He still couldn't drive yet, his arm was in a sling and he still was on pain medication, but after getting Ken's call, he knew he needed to reach the restaurant fast.

The moment he noticed the Closed sign on the door, his heart dropped. Ken wouldn't close the restaurant except in an emergency. Something was really bad, but he'd fix it. He always did. Too bad he couldn't say the same about his love life. He hadn't heard from Caryn in nearly a week, but he couldn't think about her right now. His business needed him.

Adrian rushed inside and headed for the kitchen.

"The problem's not there," Ken said, resting an arm around Adrian's shoulders and steering him towards to the dining area.

Adrian looked at his friend, surprised by his formal attire—a dark suit with a yellow flower. "What's go—"

He didn't have a chance to finish when he noticed the dining hall decorated with white and yellow ribbons, glass bowls bursting with small yellow bouquets nestled on white tablecloths. He started to grin. Had Ken set up a Welcome Back Party? But he didn't see a banner. And he couldn't understand why Caryn's friend, Terri, was standing there wearing a cream colored dress, and her sister and brother. And why was his sister also dressed up and looking near tears? What were all the flowers for? Then he noticed the small arch lined with yellow roses, and a woman in a business suit standing underneath it as if ready for a ceremony...

His heart stopped when the music began to play.

The wedding march.

It couldn't be.

He spun around and saw Caryn slowly walking towards him dressed in a bright yellow gown with tiny white accents, a small bouquet of roses in her hand.

Adrian glanced down at his jeans and sneakers in dismay then glared at Ken. "Why didn't you warn me?"

"She wanted this to be a surprise," Ken said without apology.

He looked back up at his bride as she approached him, his heart dancing with joy. She was coming to him. Her aunt hadn't kept them apart and she couldn't interfere again. She would finally be his completely. He'd won.

Caryn stopped in front of him, looking a little embarrassed. "I wanted to be your yellow bird." She looked down at her dress. "But is it too much yellow?"

It was blindingly yellow. Wonderfully yellow. She was his sun. Something that could cast away all the dark clouds of his life.

He lifted her chin. "It's perfect." He bent down to kiss her.

Ken hit him on the back. "You get to do that after the ceremony."

A ceremony that was small in attendance but big on love, their guests cheering, crying and laughing when the couple finally said 'I do'. They kissed and everyone else faded away as they were briefly swept back to an autumn night on a balcony with the moon bright overhead, wrapped up in a magic that had a name all its own, and then swept forwards years into the future where they renewed their vows one spring afternoon in front of their children and grandchildren.

When they finally pulled apart, Caryn gazed up at the man who was now her husband, knowing she'd found her own true love. A man who'd once been a dashing, dark stranger who now filled every corner of her heart.

She turned to the small crowd, lifted up her dress and gave them a peek of the yellow fishnets she was wearing, which had given her the idea for her dress. While everyone was enjoying the cake Ken had made, she looked up, and through the large restaurant window she saw Rita across the street. The woman who'd helped her to dream of second chances again.

Caryn raced outside as Rita headed to a gray Acura and called out her name.

Rita smiled at her and waved, but didn't stop. Instead she jumped into her car and drove away. Caryn blinked when she saw her license plate: STCKIGS.

Adrian came out and joined her, a look of worry on his face. "What's wrong, CeCe?"

She watched the car disappear into traffic, then stared up at him, her gaze brimming with happiness."Nothing," she said, cupping his face. "Nothing at all."

ABOUT THE AUTHOR

Dara Girard, an award-winning, national bestselling author of more than forty novels, from romance to suspense, loves telling stories.

Born in the US to immigrant parents, Dara enjoys pulling from her Jamaican, British, Nigerian heritage and exposure to various cultures to bring what reviewers and fans call "vivid emotional stories" to life. She is best known for her popular Henson Series, the mysterious Clifton Sisters, and the fun Black Stockings Society.

You can write her at:
contactdara@daragirard.com
or
P.O. Box 10345
Silver Spring, MD 20914
If you'd like to receive a reply, please send a self-addressed stamped envelope.

Visit her website to sign up for her newsletter and get sneak peeks, monthly updates on new releases, and special offers.

For more information visit
www.daragirard.com